Siene

RED LIPS

Book Three of the Red Series

Red Lipstick
Hot as fire
Sexy as red satin
Delicious like a red apple
Powerful color of love
It makes men feel things and squirm
Awakes their hormones and drags them in

By Gabi Gabriella

RED LIPS

Leonard Di Gregorio

Cover designed by Cover Designer Guzel Studio

This book is a work of fiction. Names, characters, places, and incidents either are products of the author's imagination or are used fictitiously. Any resemblance to actual persons, living or dead, events, or locales is entirely coincidental.

Leonard Di Gregorio
Visit my website at www.ldigregorio.com

Printed in the United States of America

First Printing: March 2020
Bailey- Webster Publishing

ISBN-13 978-1-7331917-3-9

This book is dedicated to my best friend, Thomas Walker. Remembering all the crazy things we tried together. The one who will always be there when I need him.

ACKNOWLEDGMENT

I want to acknowledge the support of my wife, Barbara, and my two wonderful daughters, Danielle and Michelle, who were invaluable in finalizing this manuscript.

A special thank you to Roger Quinn, mentor, editor, and friend, who led me on this path I never thought I would take.

Thank you, Rich Gale, my story editor, for your guidance.

To my Eight Chairs Writers Group for your support and patience.

And of course, my beta readers, Caroline (Tinker) Frazier, Kathy Hughes, and Linnea Knecht, who correct all my mistakes.

CONTENTS

PROLOGUE

Gulf of Mexico 22⁰ 06" 36' N by 84⁰ 37" 41' W

Somedays you should just stay in bed.

The monotonous drone and the soft rolling of the *Thumbs Up* lulled Michael Summerfield into a delusional state. He left Key West yesterday, looking at the blue sky, yearning to get on the ocean and complete the final measurement of the angle of the stars on the horizon. Checking his chronometer and charts, he calculated his position. There was a slight deviation. Adjustments made. Still approximately 20 nautical miles from Arroyos de Mantua, Cuba, two days away from his destination, Cancun. Last night's argument distressed him.

There wasn't enough money in the world to satisfy her hunger. Enough is enough. I have to live. He thought to himself.

The next morning an orange sun splashed through the window of his cabin. A hatch led to the engine compartment, where

Michael checked the oil. It was still full. The repairs made in Key West were holding.

Later in the day, Michael noticed cumulus clouds gathering on the horizon. They were heading his way. The sky grew darker as the hours passed. Cumulonimbus cloud formations formed a black anvil foretelling what was ahead. *It looks like I'm in for nasty weather.* By noon the sky was the color of a glass of Cabernet.

A drop of rain appeared on the windshield. Another followed. Soon it became a deluge. Rocking back and forth, he was thankful he was not on the flying bridge. But seeing through the windshield was difficult. Soon the wipers cleared the view. The seas became bloodthirsty with treacherous waves smashing against the sides of the boat. It forced Michael to change course and head directly into the perilous waves before they rolled the ship. Between fighting the waves and the strong current attempting to push him east towards Bermuda, he was losing precious time. But safety was paramount. Time is just minutes to make up, but life is final.

Pushing the throttle forward to increase speed resulted in sputtering sounds below deck. A quick check below identified the issue. After opening the hidden hatch, he pulled the lever and switched tanks. Problem solved.

Thumbs Up continued. Time passed, and Michael checked his chronometer watch. He found only minutes passed and not the hours he hoped for. A heavy mist interfered with his vision. The winds kept getting stronger. It was difficult controlling the vessel. Michael rushed to the outside locker and retrieved one of the life jackets. *What was that?* The dinghy he strapped to the back of the handrail broke loose. As he fought his way over and through the howling wind, Michael started to secure the dinghy.

RED LIPS

Without warning, the engine exploded. The force catapulted Michael overboard. For a moment, he was in shock. *Where am I? What just happened?* He was alone floating in the ocean. Ahead of him was the *Thumbs Up. Just get back to the boat. Swim as fast as you can.* But the ship started listing. Waves rushed over its side. It was floundering. Michael watched as it vanished under the surface of the sea. He lost hope. *Fuck, why didn't I get the life jacket earlier?... What's that?* The dinghy. The little boat dislodged and was still afloat. He swam towards it. The rough seas kept pushing the dinghy away. He seemed to get nowhere. *I'll never make it. I'll drown in this shit ocean.* He stopped and floated. *Hell no, I'm not finished. I'll go down fighting.* The battle resumed. *Stroke...stroke...stroke.* With every ounce of his strength, he reached the dinghy. He hung on its side, exhausted, trying to catch his breath. After a short rest, he pulled himself on board. Exhausted, he lay on the deck. It took a full hour before he regained his strength.

What went wrong? He checked the complete electrical and fuel systems when he arrived in Key West and made the repair for the oil leak. Everything was in perfect order then. He did not tamper with or use the boat until he left.

Michael recalled that day at the marina. Maria, his daughter, promised not to tell anyone where he was going, but her mother surprised him. "Please sell the damn patent; we need the money," she demanded. He refused and the fight began. *It was none of her business why I wouldn't sell the patent. That's when the fireworks started. But would she sabotage my boat and kill me? Perhaps.*

Although Michael was in the dinghy, there was fear in his eyes. Without oars or food and water to drink, he was at the whim of

3

nature's wrath. *I wonder if my cell phone is still working.* But he remembered he left it in the cabin. The storm passed. Michael drifted, lost under the blistering Caribbean sun.

Michael was sure he was going to die. No one would find him in his little dinghy in this vast ocean. *My life has been one fiasco after another. I end my life as a failure. If only I could see my precious little girl once more. I guess Marie's not a little girl anymore. She's a young lady.* He had nothing but time to look back on his life. His career was a flop. After years of working for the same company, he was let go without a pension. One failed marriage and another going the same way, at least he had a beautiful daughter with the first. *Dorothy, my first wife, always focused on the family. Perhaps that was my mistake, focusing on a career instead.* There was no chance with the second. *My second wife, Suzanne, is no better, she's only interested in her business. But I can't tell her why I refused to sell my patent.* There was nothing left but wait for the inevitable.

Michael saw the fishing line stuck in the boat's bottom. *What's this? Hope? Perhaps?* He emptied his pockets. The Swiss Army knife he carried since he was a scout came out. In the other pocket, he found the two paperclips he had thrown in when he cleared the kitchen counter. A plastic garbage bag stuck in his back pocket to use in the bathroom trash can. Moments later, he formed a crude hook with the clip. But he had no bait or sinker — *the ring.* Michael pulled off his wedding band and tied it by the hook. *Maybe a fish will notice its sparkle in the water and take a bite.* He tied one end of the line to the boat, then dropped the other down into the sea.

RED LIPS

The sun beat on him. He needed shade. Removing his shirt and crouching in the dinghy's bow, he draped the shirt over his head and shoulders. There was no drinkable water. *How long can a man go without water? Five days, perhaps a week at most.* He did not want to think about it. It only made things worse.

That night it poured for fifteen minutes. Mike pulled out the garbage bag, slicing the side open with his knife it became a sheet. He draped the sheet over the back of the boat. Mike saved a few mouthfuls of water. The second day he was still skunked. *No fish today.* Again, no rain.

On the third day, his lips blistered. The shirt he used to cover his shoulders and head still exposed parts of his body to the sun. Blisters appeared. Realizing this might be his last day alive, he turned to God.

Kneeling, he said aloud, "God, religion has never been important to me. But if you help me get out of this mess. I will start going to church."

Michael checked his line. It was the same as always. *Lord, if you will give me one more chance, I will change my ways. I will try my best. There will not be a day without the Lord in my mind and spirit. I will take the path you give me. Each day I will have you by my side, showing me the way to be a better person.*

Time passed, but nothing changed. This day would end soon. Michael knew tomorrow might never come. Finally, he pleaded and screamed, "God, let me live."

Michael rubbed his sunburned eyes. Something was in the distance. There, a small fishing boat. He struggled to stand and attempted to yell out, but his throat was so dry he could not speak. He desperately grabbed the shirt with one hand and the plastic bag with the other and started waving his arms. The boat started toward Michael.

A stranger grabbed Michael and helped him into the boat. Michael hugged the man and kissed him before he passed out.

CHAPTER ONE

The Hook

"Are you dead?"

Tom Walker sprawled, unfettered, across a cheap, green plastic deck lounger, laid out like a fish waiting to be fileted. Squinting beneath the brim of his knock-off captain's hat, his Ray-Ban sunglasses protected his eyes and identity. That dirty white cap covered his wispy grey hair.

He casually surveyed the shoes and sandals, supporting pretty feet and shapely legs as they passed him.

Shirtless under the full Mexican sun, a soggy Montecristo cigar dangled crushed between his left-hand fingers. The cigar burned out long ago. His right hand pointed toward an empty Corona bottle unspun in a pool of spilled beer. Sandals dangled from his feet. His red and green striped bathing trunks barely protected his manhood. Not so his bulbous stomach nor his hairy chest that had grown hoary over the years.

That's nice, he mused. An odor passed by or was it? No, a scent. Yes, very lovely, he inhaled, enjoying the whiff. Or was it?

No, more than an extraordinary scent. A fragrance. His memory reeled in the alluring smell as if it were a sailfish on a very long line. He could feel it pulling, breaking through, jumping, flashing light, as he pulled and reeled in a familiar scent from long ago. One that caused him to remember a sensual experience with Chanel No. 5.

A leg peeking through a slit skirt appeared in his right eye. Excellent, very nice. A burp sounded. Standing before him on the dock was a woman wearing red stiletto heels, shapely calves, legs slightly apart. He had to lift his hat to see the rest of this magical apparition. Staring at him through dark sunglasses, he could barely make out his own uncomely appearance.

Tom surveyed the tall, slender figure, with onyx hair. The bobbed haircut curled under her cheeks, framing her face. *Not bad on the eyes.* A large red flopping hat that protected her ivory face matched her bright red lipstick that accentuated her full lips. Professional model? Perhaps.

"Are you talking to me?" asked Tom as he opened both eyes.

"Yes. If this is the *My Fortune* and you're Captain Tom Walker?"

Tom's eyes stared through her white linen halter top and sheer sarong at her captivating breasts and thighs.

"That's what they call me," responded an intrigued Tom Walker.

"Then, yes, I'm looking for you," she stated in that silky voice.

A breeze awakened, and she casually held her hat as a wisp of hair floated across those substantial tantalizing red lips.

Tom felt arousal from an old friend finally brought back to life. One he had not felt in years. *This broad had looks and the money to show it off.* He fumbled, trying to get off the lounger and stumbled onto the rear deck of *My Fortune.*

"Give me a second. Must have had too much sun," said Tom as he reached for the cigar that had fallen out of his hand at least three times before he picked it up.

Tom made it into the galley and splashed some water on his face. He reached for a bottle of mouthwash on the shelf, took a swig, gargled and spit it out. After straightening his sixty-two-year-old body, he passed by a mirror. A quick survey revealed a little paunch at his middle. He sucked in his stomach and marched out to the deck.

"Sorry about that. How can I be of service?" He started a new conversation with the enticing stranger.

"The sign on the dock says Captain Thomas Walker, Charters by appointment only. I'm here to make an appointment."

"Well, come into my office, and we can discuss it."

Tom extended his hand and assisted this mysterious woman aboard the swim platform of *My Fortune,* his 57-foot Riviere Sport Fisherman yacht. He stepped aside and waved his hand, directing her toward the transom door.

"Let me help you up to the deck." offered Tom.

She took his hand, and grandiosely stepped onto the rear teak deck.

"I think it's too hot out here. Let's go into the salon where it's cooler."

As she stood there, Tom looked directly at her lips. *She's tall. Taller than me. My kind of woman.*

"Why don't we take a seat on the corner sofa?" asked Tom

"Thank you."

The opera *Carmen* played softly in the background.

"What kind of charter are you looking for? Fishing, perhaps?"

She placed her sunglasses on the table and looked directly at him, sizing him up with her large amber eyes. "I heard you were a person who had experience locating missing items?"

I can't take my eyes off her lips. Those pouting red, full Betty Grable lips; lips that beg to be kissed. And I'm the man to do it.

"Where did you hear that?" asked Tom rolling his eyes.

"From people around the area."

"They tend to exaggerate, but I guess that's true." Tom continued, wanting to keep her on the hook.

For a moment, Tom contemplated his next move. Finally, he asked, "What are you looking for?"

"My husband."

CHAPTER TWO

The Line

A few years back, Tom Walker and his friends found a sunken treasure ship off the coast of Florida. Since retiring on his new yacht, *My Fortune,* in Puerto Aventuras, Mexico, the story had spread. Over time, it had been exaggerated.

Of course, he was a few years older. He still had his wispy grey hair, but perhaps not quite as much. His features had not changed, although he did add the white grey handlebar mustache and another ten pounds to his original one hundred sixty-pound frame.

"You have a beautiful view from here," said the woman with the red lipstick. "I see many charters are leaving this morning. Why are you still here?"

"They need the money. I don't."

"That's extraordinary. I would think this yacht of yours and the docking fee would cost a fortune."

"They do."

"But when do you go out on charters?"

"When I get bored."

"I am sorry. It's none of my business, but I must ask. How do you keep this lifestyle?"

"Why?"

"Because I deal only with honest people."

"Reasonable. I received over eight million dollars from a treasure I found."

"Then why the sign? You apparently don't need the work."

Tom walked over to the bar and poured himself a tumbler of Irish Whiskey. He offered one to his prospect, but she refused any alcohol.

"Can I get you an iced tea?"

"Yes, that would be fine. But you haven't answered my question."

He poured a tea and placed it on the table. "I don't want to feel useless. Needed a purpose."

He took a seat across from her.

"Now that you have interrogated me, it's my turn. Who are you?"

"Suzanne Summerfield," she replied, hiking up her skirt just enough to entice Tom.

Perhaps things were looking up.

"Is it Sue or Susan?" inquired Tom.

"Suzanne."

"Very well, Suzanne. Let's get down to business. What's this all about?"

She hesitated, searching for a tissue in her purse, "My husband, Michael, is missing. I haven't heard from him in weeks."

"But why are you looking here in Puerto Aventuras?"

"Let me start again. Michael had been an automotive engineer for General Motors designing combustion engines. His task was to find a means to increase gas mileage to comply with future EPA standards. Two years ago, after discovering a formula to use seawater to improve gas mileage, he was fired."

"Fired? Why I would have thought they would be ecstatic."

"So did he, but they wanted to shelve the idea. There was a disagreement about proceeding. He left the company. But since then, he developed an engine using his patent. That's all I know."

"Impossible. They still haven't found a way to turn shit into gold. You want me to believe he changed water into gasoline. Even Jesus Christ didn't try that one."

Tom was still laughing when she continued.

"I don't know about changing water into gasoline. He just invented an engine that ran on water instead of gas. Michael replaced the engine in his boat with his new design and decided to show them up by motoring his boat from Newport to Cancun, using two gallons of gas."

"That is a long trip for a motorboat."

"I know, but Michael insisted on going."

"Where is he now?"

She placed the tissue to her eyes, patting away the tears. Looking down, she moved her head side to side and continued, "I don't know. He would call every day letting me know he was safe and where he was. But... then the calls stopped. It's been two weeks."

"So, he had a satellite phone."

"Yes, I demanded he carry one in case of an emergency."

"Have you notified the police?"

"Yes, all they did was send a wire to all the islands. I don't believe this is high on anyone's priority list but mine."

"Where was he when you last heard from him?"

"Key West. He was heading for Cancun, Marina Hacienda Del Mar."

"Suzanne, this is out of my line. It's been lovely chatting with you, but you need a private detective."

"No, I need you. I'll pay whatever you ask." Still wiping her tears, she continued, "I don't know what I would do if something happened to Michael. I begged him not to go. I told him it was too dangerous, being out in that ocean alone with an experimental engine, but he wouldn't listen. You've got to help me."

She bent over. Tom placed his palm over her clutched hands.

"Alright, let me think about it overnight. I'll give you a call tomorrow with my decision."

She opened her purse and traded her tissue for a small notepad. After scribbling something, she handed it to Tom. "Here's my cell number."

Tom placed the paper in his pocket.

"Please, I'll be waiting for your call."

Tom took Suzanne by the hand and assisted her off the *My Fortune*. He gazed at her as she walked down the dock. He couldn't take his eyes off her. Not until that tight ass was out of sight. *I wonder what else she's looking for?*

CHAPTER THREE

The Sinker

L ater that evening, after a change of clothes, Tom leisurely walked past the other boats and condos to the center of the small shopping area located on the edge of the marina. There were bars, restaurants, and gift shops. That's where the nightly activities happened. An alcove in this area contained the dolphin pens. A company appropriately named Dolphin Discovery, provided daily dolphin experiences for the tourists. He enjoyed watching the show from the restaurant across the way.

Papacito's Cocina Mexicano was one of Tom's favorites, and he sauntered in and took a seat at his usual place at the end of the bar. A piece of string lay on the counter. Tom started toying with it.

The restaurant was open to the weather. A pleasant breeze swept by. Tom smelled the fragrance of Mexican orange blossoms in the air. An opaque fiberglass roof, supported by six wooden poles, gave comfort and shade from the sun.

He watched two couples laughing at today's dolphin experience, which they had just completed. One spectator with his hands raised high in the air, was discussing the best technique to rise out of the water during the dolphin push.

Manuel Sanchez, or Manny as his friends called him, owner and bartender, placed the usual Corona with lime and a bowl of chips with red and green salsa in front of Tom. *That should keep Tom busy for a while,* as he moved on to other patrons ordering the more expensive entrees on his menu. Tom took a sip and scanned the room. *I haven't left Puerto Aventuras in over two years. Perhaps, it is time for a change of scenery. My Fortune* became Tom's nest, and he was reluctant to leave the coop.

"Good evening, Captain Walker." Manny looked down at the bar top and asked, "What's that? A string? Are we starting a crocheting class?"

As Tom looked up, he answered, "Just found it lying on the counter. Look, this is Cat's Cradle. Do you remember playing that as a child?"

"No, never got into that one."

"How about the Star?"

"No string tricks. We didn't have the time in my hood."

"Sorry about that. I will teach you someday."

"If you say so. What'll we be feasting on this evening?"

"Manny, I think I will partake in one of your delicious chicken quesadillas."

Manny grew up in New York and had absolutely no Mexican accent. He had to fake it for the tourists, but he knew better than to try it with Tom.

After placing the order, the conversation continued, "Captain Tom, I don't get it. You're one of the richest people I know, and you always order the cheapest thing on the menu."

"Besides being frugal, it's probably the best thing on your menu," Tom answered with a smile. "I think I'll be taking a trip for a short period. Perhaps I'll have some excellent food then."

"Who ya kiddin'? You haven't left that stool in over a year."

"No! Really. I accepted an impromptu audacious endeavor that will require my perspicacious methods of deduction. Hence I will be leaving this seat for some time."

"You're at it again, Walker, using those hifalutin words. Must I remind you that I didn't get that Rutgers University Masters in English you did? I just graduated from the local community college. Now tell me in plain English."

"Pardon me, Manuel, I have accepted a spur-of-the-moment adventure to locate a missing person who requires my shrewd methods of deduction."

"So you're a Private Investigator. Who'd hire you?"

"No! I'm not a P.I., but a beautiful woman with red lipstick insisted I take the case to locate her missing husband. And she's going to sweeten the pot with a large sum of money. Real money, U.S. dollars, not those pesos that keep losing their value."

"What girl with red lipstick?"

"Oh, never mind. I think I can do it. It's worth a try. Besides, the woman aroused me for the first time in years."

"But, she's married."

"Well… perhaps… a widow."

The bell rang from the kitchen, the banter between Tom and Manuel ended. Manuel brought Tom his quesadilla.

Soon a buxom platinum blond sauntered by giving Tom a pinch on his rump.

"Hi, Beverly," said Tom discretely.

17

Beverly Mount, tall with beached platinum blond hair, was trying to imitate Marilyn Monroe. *Well, I guess this would be how Marilyn would have looked by now if she hadn't already passed on.* Bev had the hooters, at 42 inches at least, to go with the image. At 70 years of age and widowed for the past ten years, she was the local cougar on the prowl.

Sliding onto a stool beside Tom, she asked, "Tommy, why don't you ever sit at a table?"

"It attracts guests."

"Sometimes…I don't know if you're kidding with me. Perhaps another time?"

"Sure," quipped Tom taking a forkful of quesadilla.

Beverly found a table in the back with an unaccompanied tourist.

He had just finished his dinner, and Manny was clearing the counter when another local, Sammy Sharp, strutted in and occupied the seat beside Tom.

"Hi, Tom…Manny," announced Sammy in a loud squeaky voice.

Manny waved a hand and said, "Time for me to leave."

"Tom, did I tell you about the blue marlin I caught last month? It was at least five hundred pounds. Fought me for three and a half hours before I was finally able to get her on board."

"Sammy, you lie more than a fiction writer."

"I don't lie," answered Sammy as he puffed out his chest.

"Then let's call it what it is. You embellish. Remember, I was there with you, and that marlin weighed nowhere near a hundred pounds. More like fifty, and you never got it on the boat."

"Oh yeah, I forgot. By the way, did that luscious brunette find you?"

"So, you told her I could locate her husband?"

"Well, you did find the treasure."

"How many times do I have to tell you, it was my partners, Cas, Holly, and Shaun that found the treasure. I just captained the boat. I couldn't find the ring on a donut, let alone a hidden treasure in an open sea."

"Well, I was trying to help. That's the thanks I get for helping a friend. After all, she was a knockout. By the way, did you get the job?"

"Sorry to say, yes, I did."

"See what I did for you. Perhaps you'll get lucky with this one."

"No way, she's married."

Manny returned with Tom's check. Tom reached into his pocket and left a sawbuck.

Tom wandered back to *My Fortune.* He had a buzz on and just plopped on his bed, clothes and all. He would plan the adventure tomorrow.

CHAPTER FOUR

Landed

Tom's head was pounding the next morning. *My Fortune* kept rocking back and forth. He peeped through the window curtains and realized a tropical storm had become his alarm clock, thunder, and lightning his wake-up call. Still in last night's clothes, he undressed, dumped them in the wash, and marched into the shower. Coldwater splashed over his body, rinsing the cobwebs out of his head. Next, to get things back together. As he stared in the mirror, he tried to remember last night. *Yesterday... Let's see... I was drinking beer and smoking a cigar — the woman. Oh, yeah, I fell in love and was about to accept a new job.*

The pot started to gurgle as Mr. Coffee completed its task. Tom poured himself a mug and headed out on deck just as the rain subsided. *Just another one of those Mexican fifteen-minute showers.* He sipped coffee and watched his friend Fidel passing through the canal on his boat. Tom waved. Fidel was one of the charter fleet's captains, leaving every morning with their clients hoping to catch a tarpon. They had jobs to do. Hard but gratifying. Well, now he had a job.

But why? Absentmindedly pulling the string out of his pocket, he fiddled with it between his fingers. He didn't need the money, couldn't spend all that he had. Can't complain about lounging around on a beautiful yacht drinking beer in this beautiful tropical paradise.

He had plenty of friends. All the bartenders from Playa del Carmen to Tulum knew him by name. Was it the challenge… perhaps? But he did not need the assignment to have an adventure. He could take *My Fortune* out on his own. No, it was her. He was snagged. She was forbidden fruit, and he wanted to take a bite of the apple. *I get aroused just thinking about her.* The string went back in his pocket.

The cell only rang twice before Suzanne answered, "Hello."

"Suzanne, it's Tom Walker. I'll accept your offer."

"Wonderful," Suzanne answered in that deep silky voice Tom found so attractive. "When can you start?"

"Well, I'd like to come over and get some information this afternoon."

"No, I have some errands to run. How about I meet you at, say around four at the marina?"

"Do you have a dinner engagement this evening?" asked Tom.

"No."

"Great, let's make it around 5 p.m. at Papacito's Cocina."

"Fine. See you there."

The rain stopped, the sun appeared, and the clouds melted away. Tom loved the scent of the air after a rainstorm. He inhaled it. The sweet, pungent clean smell of the air made Tom remember when he first came to Puerto Aventuras. Then there was never enough time in the day. He was always on the go. But not anymore. Now it was the same every day. Drink all day on the yacht, Manny's for dinner, and return to the boat drunk. Repeat. The other people were living on their boats. But they had lived. They were going out dancing, playing golf or tennis. He was invited to their parties but never accepted. *I need to get that exhilarating feeling back. Perhaps, a stroll would help.*

Tom started by strolling through the Omni Puerto Aventuras Ocean Resort. As he passed the front desk, he waved to his friend, Gerry. Outside was the hotel's restaurant overlooking Puerto Aventuras' beautiful white sandy beach. Condos and homes had replaced the open spaces along the beach. He mused about the old days when he could walk this part of the beach and see no one for miles.

A few minutes later, he was walking outside the marina area. He stopped at the white gazebo. *I wonder if the mariachis still play here on summer nights.*

A small dog ran up to him, and he leaned over to pet him. It reminded him of his dogs, Mandy, Jasmine, Jack, and Harley, long since gone.

"G' day, mate. Where have you been."

"Hi, John. I guess hibernating on my boat. I decided to take a walkabout. Is that a new dog I see?" asked Tom.

"Charlie. Ye, he's a little Micky I found wandering around. He's been following me ever since."

"Micky, I don't know that one."

RED LIPS

"You know… a young stray calf. Just what you need to get you out and about."

"Not at this time. On the boat, dogs are impractical."

"Excuses Tom, just excuses," said John as Charlie pulled him away.

A small pastry shop on the corner beckoned Tom with its tantalizing aromas. Quanita called out, "Mr. Tom, so good to see you. Come sit down with me."

Quanita's Coffee House served the best pan dulce (sweetbreads) on the Riviera Maya.

"Not today, Quanita. But I will have one of your sweet cheese-filled sopapilla and a coffee to go — *Por favor.*"

While she prepared his breakfast, she asked, "Where have you been? You never stop by anymore."

"I've passed several times, but you're always crowded," he lied. It was over two years since he traveled this far from the boat.

"Yes, we are swamped. Many new condos on the golf course with many tourists."

"Good for you. Bad for me," replied Tom as he left with his breakfast.

There was a golf course where he played regularly every Monday and Thursday. It was not a championship course, but it worked for his game. But he had not played in the last two years. *I should get back to playing again.* He strolled back to *My Fortune* and dressed for his meeting with Suzanne.

He found his favorite shirt. The one he bought in Hawaii too many years ago to remember the date. But he was still married then. *Hawaiian shirts never go out of style. Do they?* "Damn I look good."

Tom took his usual seat at the bar and ordered a vodka martini with three olives for luck. The tables were still empty. Too early for the tourists. It was past five, and Suzanne had not arrived, but Beverly had.

"Hi, Tom, come sit by me in the corner."

"No can do. Got a client. Sorry," he replied.

"I don't see anyone sitting by you."

"She's not here yet."

"Well, if she stands you up, you know where I'll be," said Beverly as she sashayed to a far table.

"*Sure.*" Tom said to himself.

Beverly stared at Tom with longing. *I wonder why he hasn't taken me up on my numerous offers. I don't think I look bad for my age. I look damn good. Tom is no spring chicken either. He's never been with a woman the whole time I've known him. Let's see, that's about two years. Perhaps he's gay.*

Tom was contemplating another martini. Just then, something eclipsed the sun.

Suzanne arrived, still wearing the bright red lipstick. She was all in red, red floppy hat protecting her ivory face from the sun and a coordinated red sheath dress with a slit up the side that did not hide much of her red panties.

She walked past Tom and pointed to a table in the back.

Tom followed her like a puppy, mesmerized. The dress accentuated every nook and cranny begging to be explored.

RED LIPS

Suzanne slid gracefully into the seat with her back to the wall and faced the open entrance. She removed her hat and placed it on a chair. Her shoulder-length black hair curled in at the bottom revealing her passion.

Oh! Yes, and the scent of Chanel No. 5.

"I'm so pleased you decided to accept my offer. What can I do to help you find my Michael?"

"Well, first of all, I need a recent photo, more than one if you have them."

Opening her red handbag, she removed a glossy photo of Michael standing on the back of his boat, the *Thumbs Up*. He was wearing a sky blue t-shirt, long white linen trousers, tied at the waist with a cord. Michael had medium-length salt and pepper hair.

"I guess he's about six feet, 190 pounds."

"No, six-four and 200 pounds," she corrected.

"This was taken on our last vacation. We motored along the New England coastline. Stayed at a charming bed-and-breakfast in Marblehead."

"Is this the boat he was on at the time of his disappearance?"

"Yes, it's a 2015 43 Carver coupe," answered Suzanne.

"That's a treacherous trip for a boat that size."

"Oh, he's made the trip to the Keys many times."

"Perhaps, but he would be hugging the coast and using the Intracoastal Waterways. He would be challenged in the open seas with that size boat."

"Do you think the boat sank? Oh please, don't say that." She reached in her purse and pulled out the hankie again.

"Not necessarily. I have known smaller boats making it. It just would not be a pleasant trip. We shall go on the assumption he is still alive."

"Thank you, Captain Tom."

He placed his hand on her shoulder, "Just Tom, please."

"Walker. You guys gonna order something or take up space? I ain't got all night." Manny arrived at the table.

"Yes. Give us a second. We just got here," said Tom.

"Alright already."

"Manny, this is Ms. Suzanne Summerfield."

"*Mrs*. Summerfield," Suzanne corrected.

"Glad ta meet ya," Manuel answered.

"Do I detect a New York accent, Manny?" quizzed Suzanne.

"Got me. I'm from New York."

"How did you wind up down here?"

"ICE raids. But that was long ago. Things are better now."

"I'm glad to see someone made it out of those raids. I guess that makes you unique in this area."

"How's that?" asked Manny

"A Mexican with a New York attitude."

"Yeah, I guess you're right. Are you ready to order?"

"Yes, do you have any sparkling water?" Suzanne asked.

"Topo Chico or San Pellegrino."

"I'll have the San Pellegrino with ice, a wedge of lime, and a large house salad. And instead of dressing, just some balsamic vinegar on the side."

"I'll have the steak fajitas and another martini," added Tom.

RED LIPS

They continued the conversation regarding how to locate Michael. Tom realized Suzanne would be strictly business.

"Tell me about Michael's boat."

"Yes. The *Thumbs Up* is a forty-three foot, 2015 Carver Coupe yacht, as I already told you. It's all white with twin 480 horsepower Cummins engines."

"Where did you last hear from him?"

"Key West. He said he was leaving for Cancun. That was two weeks ago. He hasn't called since."

"What day was that?"

"April 30," said Suzanne glancing at her cell phone.

"Did he have a specific route he was taking to Cancun?"

"All I know is he was going there from Key West. He didn't give any information on how."

"Well, I guess Cancun is the place to start."

The meal continued for two hours. Tom kept the conversation going with his rhetorical style of speech. Suzanne had enough chit chat. She stood up and placed her hat on her head, looked at Tom, and said, "I'll be leaving for Newport first thing tomorrow morning. Call me when you have something." She removed a check from her wallet and handed it to Tom. "Meanwhile, take this."

"Five thousand dollars," is all a startled Tom could say.

"That should get you started. I'll send you more when needed," Suzanne turned and left the restaurant.

Tom pulled out his string and pondered. "What's next?" he said as he stroked his head with the palm of his right hand. *What would I do if I completed the trip? Celebrate! I bet Michael's carousing in some bar in Cancun right now. Perhaps with a little chica on the side. That's it, go to Cancun. Pull him out of the bar. Make an easy five G's.*

RED LIPS

STEAK FAJITAS
Start to finish: 2 hours 40 minutes

Serves 4

1/4 cup extra-virgin olive oil, plus more for cooking

Juice of 1 lime

1 teaspoon dried oregano

1/2 teaspoon ground cumin

1/2 teaspoon chili powder

1 pound skirt steak

Kosher salt

Freshly ground black pepper

1 bell pepper, thinly sliced

1 large onion, sliced into half-moons

Tortillas, for serving

Sour cream, for serving

Cilantro, for serving

Salsa, for serving

DIRECTIONS
In a large bowl, whisk together olive oil, lime juice, oregano, cumin, and chili powder. Toss steak in mixture and cover bowl with plastic wrap. Refrigerate for 20 minutes and up to 4 hours.

Preheat grill to medium-high. Place a fajita pan (or cast-iron skillet) directly on hot grill and drizzle a thin layer of olive oil to coat. Add onion and bell pepper and season with salt and pepper. Cook, occasionally stirring, until veggies are soft, about 5 minutes. Remove from heat.

3. Meanwhile, shake off excess marinade from steak and season both sides with salt and pepper. Place on grill and cook to your liking, about 4 minutes per side for medium-rare. Let rest 10 minutes before slicing (against the grain!) into strips. Add sliced steak to the skillet with veggies.

4. Garnish steak and veggies with cilantro and serve immediately with tortillas, sour cream, cilantro, and salsa.

CHAPTER FIVE

Cancun

Thirty minutes north of Playa del Carmen on Highway 307 and another twenty minutes from Puerto Aventuras, at the tip of the Yucatan Peninsula sits the city of Cancun. The entire route runs along the Atlantic Ocean. An ocean only half a mile away but hidden by the Mexican jungle.

And that is where Tom's search would begin, in Cancun, a long way from his home in Puerto Aventuras. He needed transportation. For the past two years, while in Puerto, he walked to everything as much as possible. If required, there were always golf cart rentals for local travel. But he needed a real automobile to traverse around the avenues and boulevards of Cancun.

A Google search displayed several auto rental agencies, including Avis and Hertz. But, one low budget, caught his eye, USAWRECK (pronounced, *use-a-wreck*). One that fit perfectly into Tom's Scotch budget. Their special overnight rate was twenty dollars.

Not that he did not have the money for the more well-known agencies. No need spending extra money on something to use only for one day. Tom boasted of his Scottish heritage and enjoyed his reputation for being frugal that came with it. USAWRECK worked out just fine.

While in the booking process, he noticed the added fees. Tom enjoyed pressing no for liability insurance, once again pressing no for damage insurance, GPS…no, roadside service…no. He smiled as he hit the confirm button on his laptop. The final price still read twenty dollars. "Yahoo," Tom yelled.

A few calls to the Cancun marinas and Tom had set up appointments for the next day. Four marinas could accommodate a forty-foot yacht. Start with Barracuda Marina, followed by Las Perlas and Puerto Cancun, and ending at Hacienda Del Mar. A full day's work. Back by six in time for cocktails. His only problem was his transportation location.

USAWRECK was in Playa del Carmen twenty minutes up the road. He had to pick up and drop off the car at Playa del Carmen. He needed a ride.

No problem, he had a plan.

At dinner that night, Manuel set up the usual Corona with a slice of lime for Tom. It was four-thirty in the afternoon, still too early for the dinner crowd. As usual, Tom ordered the chicken quesadillas and started toying with his string.

"Starting early," Manny observed, not questioning.

"Yes, I got a busy day tomorrow."

"What's up?" asked Manny.

"That woman I was in with the other night."

"Oh! The one you were drooling over for three hours on the same entrée."

"Yes, that one. I took her case. But I need a ride tomorrow morning to Playa del Carmen to pick up a car."

"Why didn't you pick one from here instead of Playa?"

"Got a great deal, twenty dollars for the day." Tom puffed out his chest.

"From whom?" Manuel inquired, a bit skeptical.

"USAWRECK."

"You're crazier than I thought. Do you know they use wrecks? My friend rented one, and it didn't have a front hood."

"It's just for the day. How bad can it be? So, can you?" Tom continued.

"Can I what?"

"Drop me off tomorrow morning."

Manny looked up at the ceiling and shook his head. Tom waited, hoping his friend would acquiesce. Finally, it came.

"Yeah, Amigo, what time?"

"Ten-thirty tomorrow morning."

"So, where are you going that you need a car?"

"Cancun."

"What's so special about this guy? He'll show up in some bar, eventually. They all do."

"I thought the same thing, but I'm not so sure," responded Tom.

"Why not?"

"Because he was using a new engine on his boat that used water instead of gas. If that is true, there may be people who would want him and his engine to disappear. You know… foul play."

"Holy Shit! Tell me about this engine."

"Why so interested in the engine? I think it is a hoax. Never heard of anyone changing water into gas."

"Because in 2008, I was a student of Paul Pantone. Pantone was the inventor of the Geet Fuel Processor," began Manny.

"Geek! What geek?"

"No! Geet, Global Environment Energy Technology. The Geet Fuel Processor changed liquids into gas and, finally, plasma."

"You are losing me, Manny."

"All right, here it is. Pantone developed a carburetor that used a mixture of approximately eighty percent water and twenty percent fuel to run a combustion engine. He did it on a lawnmower. The fuel could be any type and was just needed to prime the engine. Once the engine started running, it theoretically would continue running on the water vapors that changed into plasma."

"I thought plasma was what they use in hospitals?" It still puzzled Tom.

"Plasma is the fourth of six new matters discovered since you were in school. They are solid, liquid, gas, plasma, Bose-Einstein condensate (created in 1995), and the fermionic condensate created in 2004."

"Why have I never heard of this miracle?"

"Because Pantone refused to sell his patent to anyone who would not use it to improve humanity. He was offered millions by major companies who just wanted to shelve the project. They took him to court, stating he was crazy."

"Who took him to court?" asked Tom

"The oil industry. He went to a mental institution after the courts agreed with the oil companies. But he was diagnosed with cancer. The hospital released him, thinking he had only months to live. Surprise, he lived for another eight years."

RED LIPS

"So, you think this Mr. Summerfield is using that engine?"

Manuel continued, "I don't know, never heard of anyone using the technology on a full-size engine. But, if Summerfield was traveling all those distances over water using mostly water instead of gasoline, he perfected the technology much further. There's a theory that you could use junk, such as plastic instead of water. Something, like the fuel they used in the flux capacitor in *Back to the Future II*."

Tom had enough to drink and information. Beverly, the cougar, had just walked in and was on her way towards Tom.

He stood up and staggered out the door.

"See you tomorrow morning, Amigo," yelled out Manny.

CHAPTER SIX

USAWRECK

The next morning, Tom arrived at the cantina and looked for Manuel. He finally located Manuel at the rear, smoking a Marlboro, while resting on a red moped.

"Manny. Where's your car?"

"In the shop. Getting a brake job."

"How are you going to get me to Playa?"

Manuel grabbed the handlebars and slung his leg over the seat of the moped and announced, "Come on."

"Never, do I look like a child?"

"Good Mexican transportation, Amigo. If you want to get your car, I suggest you climb on. I don't have all day. I've got a business to run."

Tom hopped on the moped, and off they went. They passed the guard booth at the entrance. They continued onto Highway 307 north toward Playa del Carmen. The four-lane highway was treacherous with cars and buses moving at 70 mph.

Manuel kept shaking off Tom's arms from around his waist. Each time a bus passed, the moped shook, and Tom grabbed tighter.

RED LIPS

It did not take long before Tom's Captain's hat left his head. Flaring arms did not do the trick. The cap left forever.

The rush of passing vehicles continued until they reached the edge of Playa del Carmen. Once there, the traffic was more massive but much slower, with mopeds all over. Another scooter passed them with a man driving and a woman holding a baby on the back. Motor vehicle laws were liberal in Mexico.

Manuel pulled up in front of USAWRECK on Avenida Benito Juarez. The scent of the morning breakfast items permeated Tom's nostrils. Tacos, fruit on skewers, and deep-fried dough, called churros, were being prepared at the street corners.

Tom looked at the taxi cabs lined up at the end of the street by the town square. Their drivers assembled on the side, discussing the news of the day. Tourists jostled each other as they attempted to pass. Others window shopped on the way to the beach.

Tom started for the door, turned back, and waved. Manuel gave a casual salute back as he joined the traffic parade. He walked through the storefront and announced himself. A young boy behind the counter sported earplugs. Tom yelled, "Hello." The boy jumped up, startled. *"Hola, amigo. Que Pasa?"*

"Hola," answered Tom.

"Como Puedo ayudarle?"

"Do you speak English?"

"Si. Yes," said the boy.

"I'm here to pick up a car. Tom Walker."

"Oh, yes, Senor Walker. I have your reservation right here." The boy spoke excellent English.

"May I have your license? *Por favor.*"

Tom handed the boy his license. "Your English is excellent. Where did you learn it?"

"New Jersey. Are you familiar with the area?"

"Oh, yes, I grew up in Kearny."

"Small world, I lived in Union City until they deported me."

"Sorry about that."

"I'll be back someday. Here, sign this."

The boy took Tom out to his car, a 2016 Red Ford Fiesta.

Except for a few dents and scratches, the car looked excellent and new. He expected worse.

Tom got a quick vehicle check and instructions from the boy to be sure he filled the gas tank back up to half before he returned it. Otherwise, there would be an additional fuel surcharge. He opened the driver's side door and handed Tom the keys and said, "*Adios.*"

"*Gracias,*" answered Tom.

"*De nada,*" replied the boy returning to the office door and waving.

After getting into the car, Tom adjusted the seat and mirrors. He turned the key, and the engine started. A quick check of the traffic and the car pulled away from the curb. The drive out of town was uneventful, as he cruised down Highway 307 toward Cancun.

Tom was enjoying his favorite song, *La Mariachi Loco,* as it blasted from the radio.

It was a sunny Mexican day, and Tom thought the drive would be pleasant.

The sun decided he was wrong. Within minutes the temperature soared above ninety degrees, so Tom turned on the air conditioner. It usually took a few minutes for the interior to cool down. Tom waited and waited and waited. He placed his hand along the air ducts. The air coming in was warmer than the outside air. He checked the gauges. The heat was off, the AC was on, but still hot air. He turned it off. *I must do it the old fashioned way and open the window.*

Sliding his hand along the door panel did not reveal the magic button. There was none. A quick peek at the passenger side door revealed a hand crank for the windows. *I didn't know they still made these things.* He fiddled with the driver's side door, trying to locate the crank. There was only a nub where the handle should have been.

Trying to turn it without the handle was a struggle and impossible.

His shirt stuck to his body. He sat in a pool of water, sweat pouring off his forehead.

Tom pulled over to the side of the road. The breeze from the passing trucks was a welcome relief. He searched between and under the seats but did not locate the missing handle. *Perhaps, I can switch with the passenger side door.* Opening the passenger door, he tried but could not get it off.

Frustrated, he wrung out his shirt and laid it across the passenger seat to dry.

After another failed attempt to switch handles, Tom rolled down the passenger side window and returned to the driver's side. At least he would have some ventilation.

A pickup truck with a group of workers huddled in the truck bed passed him. They ducked down, trying to get away from the wind.

At least you have a cool breeze, Tom thought to himself.

After a few miles, he passed the pickup and pulled out. Now in the far-left lane, he made up for the lost time. A large tractor-trailer sped by Tom's right side. The wind from the passing truck almost threw Tom off the road. When he was stable again, Tom noticed his shirt being sucked out the window and flying down the road behind him.

He pulled into Cancun and located the La Isla shopping mall. Most of the tourists were still on the beaches. Parking close was no problem.

Tom exited the Fiesta or "sweatbox" as he considered it. People were looking strangely at him as he entered shirtless into the mall. He could handle it.

A directory at the entrance identified all the shops. None of the shops were recognizable to Tom. One caught his eye, Guess. *They sell jeans, don't they? That should work.*

Proceeding to the Guess store, he entered through the glass doors. Loud hip hop music played throughout the store. All the staff seemed to be very young. They wore tight jeans that appeared to have seen better days. Exposed skins showed through the rips on the knees and thighs. The seats of the jeans looked like they would not hold together much longer, either. *Perhaps they retrieved them from the local dump.*

He wondered how the store would allow that. Then he noticed the mannequins by the jeans display. The same outfit: faded blue jeans with rips at the knees. A salesclerk with spiked black and blue hair and a tie-dyed t-shirt asked if he needed help. Was he looking for something for a teenage grandson? Tom explained that he was going to a costume party and decided to go as Cheech from Cheech and Chong.

"Oh! Those Chinese detectives from the old black and white movies."

"Never mind," answered Tom, picking out a pair of white jeans.

"Do you have a changing room?"

"Yes, sir, in the back."

"By the way, do you sell underwear?" Tom asked.

"Oh, no. Only jeans and t-shirts."

Tom entered the changing room. He removed his wet underwear and socks and stuck them in the pocket of his slacks. He stepped out of the dressing room commando-style. He carried his rolled pants under his arm. As he followed the sales boy to the counter, he snagged a t-shirt, tie-dyed, of course.

The sales boy totaled out his bill. "That will be $145.95. Will you be paying cash or credit card?"

" Are you sure you got that, right? It seems like a lot for two items," asked Tom.

"Yes, sir. You're in Cancun's tourist zone. We sell only the best here."

After paying the exorbitant bill, Tom stormed out of the mall and back to the sweatbox.

On the way to Barracuda Marina, he noticed an Ace Hardware store. An idea came to him. Running in, he picked up a pair of vice grips and duct tape. He clamped the grips to the driver's side window nub. It worked. He cranked down the window, then wrapped duct tape around the vice grips. That would keep it secured until he returned to Playa del Carmen.

CHAPTER SEVEN

The Marinas

After arriving at the Barracuda Marina, he strolled the docks looking for the *Thumbs Up*. It was not there. Not that he thought it would be, but it was worth a try. The marina manager did not recognize the man in the photo nor the photo of the *Thumbs Up*. Tom thanked the man and moved on to the next marina on his list.

Las Perlas Marina was a short drive down Cancun's main drag, Avenida Kukulkan. Once again, he surveyed the yachts to no avail. The Las Perlas manager did not recognize the photos either.

Down Kukulkan to Puerto Cancun Marina, with the same results as the other two.

Hacienda Del Mar Marina was his final stop. He walked into the marina's office and asked for the manager.

"I'm sorry. We're not hiring any dock people at this time," said the receptionist as she tilted her head and shrugged her shoulders.

"I'm not looking for a job."

"Oh, I'm so sorry, but you looked like one of the seasonal dockhands."

She was not bad on the eyes. *Blond hair, a little over five feet, blue eyes, not too thin, not too heavy, and well endowed. What's not to like?*

"No problem." He handed her the photo. "Do you recognize this man?"

"No, I don't think so."

"How about the yacht?" Tom pulled out the photo of the *Thumbs Up.*

"No, but I know the name of the boat, expected her to dock here for a week back in May. It never showed. Harry, the manager, was flipping, said he turned away three other offers for a thousand dollars."

"Can I speak to Harry?"

"Sure, but he's out to lunch. Should be back soon, if you care to wait."

"Mind if I just stroll around the marina meanwhile?"

"Of course not," she said, with a smile that could melt an M&M.

Tom strolled around the docks. This was a high-end club. Most of the crafts were over thirty feet, none under twenty-six. Over the loudspeaker, he heard, "Mr. Walker, please return to the office."

Harry was waiting. A rugged man with a round brown face, close to 200 pounds, six-foot or so, blondish hair. He walked with a slight limp.

H…h-arry H…h-aug, what can I do for you, Mr. W…w-alker?"

"I'm looking for Michael Summerfield."

"He was to be here in May b…b-ut never showed."

"Did he call or give you any sign he would be late or not arrive?"

"Nope. No call, no show. Cost me a bundle. I was not happy, as y…y-ou can imagine."

"Didn't he guarantee with a credit card?"

"Y…yes, of course, b…but that was not for the full time, and there are other fees such as fuel and supplies that I would have gotten if he stayed here."

"Well, he didn't stay anywhere else; I can assure you. And from what I heard, he would not be buying much gas as he was planning on using only a gallon of gas for this trip if everything had gone as planned. He was testing a new engine. That was the purpose of his journey."

"Well, I hope he's safe."

"Thanks for your time," said Tom. As he left, he turned and winked at the receptionist. She did not return the wink.

While driving along Avenida Kukulkan, he spotted the Tourist Police Station. It was about time to check in with the local authorities. Perhaps they had found something. Tom walked into the white stucco building.

An officer glanced up from his paper as Tom approached the desk.

"How can I be of service?" asked the Officer in perfect English.

"I'm inquiring about the status of a missing person."

The officer reached into his drawer and pulled out a large pad. "Name please."

"Thomas Walker."

"And how long has Mr. Walker been missing?"

"No! He's not missing. I'm Tom Walker."

"Then why are you reporting yourself missing?"

I'm inquiring about a previous report by Mrs. Summerfield about her missing husband Michael."

"Why is she not here to make the report?" asked the officer.

Tom looked away for a moment. He scratched his head, placed his hands on the desk, and stared the officer in the eye.

"Mrs. Suzanne Summerfield was here three days ago and filled out a missing person's report for her husband, Michael Summerfield. I am here inquiring on her behalf on any progress you have made in the case."

The police officer made a call, and another officer came into the room.

"I am Captain Martinez. Come into my office."

Tom followed the Captain and took a seat in front of the desk.

"I believe you are looking into a missing person's report for a Michael Summerfield. Is that right?"

"Yes."

"How do you spell that name?"

"M-i-c-h-a-e-l S-u-m-m-e-r-f-i-e-l-d."

"And your name, please?"

"Thomas Walker."

The captain looked through some files on his desk, then typed into his computer. Tom waited patiently. There were a few glances towards Tom, by the Captain, but no conversation. A few more minutes passed, and the Captain looked at Tom and said, "There is no missing person's report filed for any Michael Summerfield. Are you sure he is missing?"

"Yes. Summerfield's wife told me she filed the report before she hired me to locate him."

"So, you are a Private Investigator. Can I see your license?"

"No, I am not a P.I. I'm just doing a favor. Perhaps she filed it at another precinct?"

"I have checked the database. There is no record of any kind. I don't believe Mrs. Summerfield filed one."

"Well, I'll file one now," Tom responded.

"What is your relationship to this Michael Summerfield?"

"What do you mean?"

"Is he part of your family? A friend? A coworker?"

"No. Nothing like that. I never met the man."

"Then I'm afraid I cannot help you. Sorry, but I think you better speak to this woman who hired you. We do not have the resources to find every drunk that gets lost after a night of tequila."

Tom was silent for the moment. An unexpected response for him.

"You're right. Sorry to waste your time. I've been duped."

"What?"

"You know, snickered, fooled, tricked."

"Oh, yes. Perhaps you are right. It was just a joke played on you. But please advise your friend we take these situations seriously."

"Thank you. I assure you I will." Tom felt his face was getting redder by the second.

Suzanne had some explaining to do. He made the call. No answer. He left a callback message.

The trip back to Puerto Aventuras took two hours with the mariachi music blasting from the radio. Still no air conditioner, but at least he could open the windows and feel the wind blowing across his face.

He arrived at Papacito's Cocina Mexicano around six in the evening. After parking and locking the car, he strolled into the restaurant. Manuel took one look at Tom and gasped. "What happened to you?"

"No AC."

"And no clothes, I see," observed Manuel.

Beverly Mount was at her usual table and eyed Tom as he entered. She gave Tom a wave. There was an enormous smile on her face.

"Love the outfit, Big Fella. Outstanding!" she shouted across the room.

Tom looked at Manny.

"What are you talking about? I just bought a completely new outfit."

"Complete, I don't think so. You ain't hide'in nuttin, partner."

"Whadda mean?" questioned an agitated Tom.

"You look like you're trolling. You forgot underwear, and wet white pants don't hide a thing."

"Oh, shit!" said Tom, looking down at his crotch. He quickly took a seat at the bar and placed a napkin over his lap.

He took a deep breath. "Can I have a tequila? Make it a double and a quesadilla. I'm famished. I haven't eaten since this morning."

RED LIPS

Beverly sauntered by as she left the restaurant and whispered in Tom's ear. "I'm ready whenever you are. If only you smelled as good as you look."

Two hours later, he stumbled out of the restaurant and made his way back to *My Fortune*. He managed to hang onto the railing when the boat began to pull away from the dock. Finally, he made his way to his stateroom.

With much effort, he finally removed his damp clothes and plopped on the bed, naked. He grabbed hold of the nightstand to keep from falling out of the spinning bed. His eyes shut, peace and blackness arrived. But not before he made three faithful decisions. He would confront Suzanne. He would go to Key West. But most of all, he would find Michael Summerfield.

LEONARD DI GREGORIO

CHICKEN QUESADILLAS

Start to finish 55 minutes

Serves: 4

1 tablespoon extra-virgin olive oil

2 bell peppers thinly sliced

½ onion, thinly sliced

Kosher salt

Fresh ground pepper

1 pound boneless, skinless chicken breasts, sliced into thin strips

1/2 teaspoon chili powder

1/2 teaspoon ground cumin

1/2 teaspoon dried oregano

4 large flour tortillas

2 cups, shredded Monterey Jack

2 cups shredded cheddar

1 avocado sliced

1 tablespoon vegetable oil

2 green onions thinly sliced

Sour cream and salsa for serving

DIRECTIONS

1. In a large skillet over medium-high heat, heat olive oil. Add peppers and onion and season with salt and pepper. Cook until soft, 5 minutes. Transfer to a plate.
2. Heat the remaining tablespoon of vegetable oil over medium-high heat. Season chicken with spices, salt, and pepper and cook, occasionally stirring, until golden and cooked through, 8 minutes. Transfer to a plate.

RED LIPS

3. Add 1 flour tortilla to skillet and top half of the tortilla with a heavy sprinkling of both kinds of cheese, cooked chicken mixture, pepper-onion mixture, a few slices of avocado, and green onions. Fold the other half of the tortilla over and cook, flipping once, until golden, 3 minutes per side. Repeat to make four quesadillas.

4. Slice into wedges and serve with sour cream and salsa.

CHAPTER EIGHT

Aerolineas Uno Dos Tres

Daybreak crept into Tom's stateroom. It took three aspirins to quiet the hammering going on in his forehead. Bending over to tie the laces on his sneakers was a challenge. It did not work. He traded them in for boat shoes.

He did make a pot of coffee, poured a cup, and sat on the deck. It was another beautiful Mexican day; blue skies dotted with big billowing puffy clouds. There were the usual afternoon showers, but they lasted only ten minutes. Tom was not looking forward to the high humidity and temperatures above ninety degrees, but still better than up north. You don't shovel sunshine.

But he still had the *sweatbox* to return. He found the Mexican national gas company, Pemex, located just down the road. They had a reputation for taking advantage of tourists.

One of their schemes was switching a 50 peso bill for a 20 and asking for more money. Tom was not going to fall for that trick. As he pulled up to the pumping station, he exited the car and announced, "Fifty Pesos, Por favor," and handed the attendant the bill.

RED LIPS

The smiling attendant just repeated, "Fifty pesos, si," and started pumping. It did not take long for the pump to reach fifty, and the gas station attendant returned the nozzle into its slot on the island dispenser. A wave of the hand and Tom was back on the road. Scanning the gas gauge, he realized the needle barely moved.

Sheepishly, he returned and requested another 100 pesos of gas. The same attendant gave him the same smile.

After dropping off the car, he took a taxi back to Puerto Aventuras, as Manny's car was still in the shop.

Yesterday had been a waste of time. Suzanne had never returned his call. He knew he had to go to Key West, the last stop before Michael became a missing person. A quick search on his iPad and he found a news flash of a new startup Mexican airline called Aerolineas Uno Dos Tres, abbreviated A123. They copied the popular business plan of the US discount carriers, Spirit and Frontier. To entice customers, they advertised a cheap fare for their inaugural service from Cancun to the US. Tom found a ticket from Cancun airport to Miami for $100 round trip.

It took a few minutes, but he finally found their website. He started entering his information, CUN-MIA. Only one flight appeared. A123's Boeing 737-600, flight number 401, leaving Cancun at 8:50 a.m. and arriving in Miami, Florida, at 11:20 a.m.

Tom accepted the flight and began the booking process. A123 offered one personal item free that must fit under the seat. Next came the à la carte options.

Do you have a carry on? (Additional cost of thirty dollars at the time of booking or sixty dollars at the gate) Tom answered, no. Do you want to buy priority boarding? (Another five dollars)

Another no. Do you want to pick your seat? (Fifteen dollars) No. Do you want to buy trip insurance? (Thirty dollars) No.

Tom chose the base package and entered his credit card information. He would leave on Monday and return on Wednesday. After confirming his choices, Tom checked off the "Have you read the A123 policy?" button and confirmed his booking. He made a copy of his receipt. He whooped when he saw the final price still read $100.

On Monday morning, at 6:50 a.m., Tom arrived at the Cancun airport. The cab was a compromise since Manuel's car was still in the repair shop, and the moped would not do. He had borrowed a small suitcase to use as his personal item, which contained a spare set of clothes and some underwear and socks. As he exited the taxi, one of the baggage porters made a grab for Tom's luggage, but Tom held tight and wheeled it in himself.

As he approached the security checkpoint, he handed the security guard his boarding pass and passport. The guard looked him over and directed him to enter the screening line.

At security, he emptied his pockets and placed his keys, cell phone and change in a plastic tray on the conveyer. Another guard advised him to put his shoes in another bin. He removed his boat shoes and followed that by setting his suitcase on the rollers. A slight push and they were on the conveyer belt that led everything through an x-ray machine that was being monitored by another security guard.

Tom started for the walk-through metal detector. Another guard asked Tom, "Please remove your hat." Tom removed the captain's hat, and he placed it on the x-ray machine belt. Alarms sounded as Tom attempted to pass. He walked through a second time with the same results. They took him aside and passed a wand over his body and gave him a pat-down.

The guard found nothing. *I fooled them. They missed my gold tooth. That's what set off the alarm. What else could they miss? Could I hide something in my crotch?* Tom smiled at the guard, revealing his gold tooth status symbol.

Proceeding to the end of the screening belt, Tom waited for his belongings to appear. The security guard stared at something on his monitor. Something stuck in the x-ray machine. A suitcase kept going back and forth.

It was Tom's suitcase. It did not fare any better after going through the x-ray machine three times.

"Are you carrying any sharp objects?" questioned the guard.

"Like what?" answered the agitated Mr. Walker.

"Knife, poker, icepick, something like that."

"Of course not. I know you can't take any weapons on an aircraft. Do you think this is my first flight? Let me tell you I've flown over 10,000 miles."

The guard picked up the tote and laid it on a side table.

Frustrated, the guard asked Tom, "Please empty your bag on the counter."

"Well, this is ridiculous," answered Tom, opening the bag.

There, for the world to see, were his socks with holes and new underwear still in the plastic wrap. They finally located a small drill that had slid under the plastic bottom of the suitcase, and Tom was free to leave. Later, Tom would find out that his friend Manny used the tote as a toolbox.

A few minutes later, he found his departure gate for his flight to Miami. Tom slid into a seat by one of the large windows that gave glimpses of the world outside. Trump had fired another of his cabinet advisors, announced the TV located on the wall. He lost count of how many and didn't know any of them. A baby screamed in the background. A man in his late nineties sat in a wheelchair looking into space and about to fall asleep. Another rotund woman sat in the corner wearing a hooded sweatshirt. The man next to him penciled numbers into a Sudoku grid.

The gate agent announced that there was a sixty-dollar charge for personal items that did not fit in the box by the counter. A public address announcement advised not to leave your luggage unattended. Some passengers just sat on the floor, playing with their cell phones.

A passenger approached the gate agent, requesting a seat change. She left in a huff after being advised of the extra charge.

Another announcement over the terminal speaker system advised, "The person who is missing their trouser belt can retrieve it at the security checkpoint."

It was 8 a.m., and the gate agent announced they were beginning the boarding process.

Tom checked his boarding pass, seat 37B, group five. First to board were the woman with her crying children followed by the man in the wheelchair. Sudoku man and the hooded woman followed. A humongous couple waddled to the gate, beads of sweat dripping from their foreheads. The gate agent announced the next group to board, "Group four may now board." The remaining cell phone users stood up from the floor and boarded.

RED LIPS

Tom was still waiting. "All remaining passengers may proceed to the podium for immediate boarding," announced the ticket agent. He picked up his bag, marched to the gate counter, and waved his boarding pass in front of the agent's face.

She calmly accepted his ticket and asked, "Mr. Walker, would you kindly place your bag in this box?" A red-faced Tom replaced the extended handle and picked up the bag by its side handle and attempted to place it in the appointed box. The handle protruded, not allowing the suitcase to fit into the box. He tried pushing it to no avail. Sitting on it did not amuse the agent. "Sixty dollars please," she announced, "and credit cards only, we don't take cash."

"You gotta be kidding?" an agitated Tom protested.

"Credit card, please," she demanded.

Tom reluctantly capitulated and handed her his credit card with Mickey Mouse on it.

Finally, he was in the aircraft aisle searching for his assigned seat. He passed row thirty-five, thirty-six, and there was the last row, thirty-seven. All the seats were full, except his place, 37B between the two who had waddled aboard.

After paying the additional sixty dollars, Tom stored his suitcase in the overhead bin. He eyed the behemoth on the aisle seat. The man rose and moved aside. Tom looked down and squeezed into the middle seat holding his breath. He located his seatbelt somewhere underneath the woman and secured himself in place. The man returned to his position.

Manufacturers did not make traditional seatbelts for certain people of massive proportions. As much as they tried, the couple could not stretch the belt far enough to reach the locking mechanism. Over the loudspeaker, the flight attendant announced, "Please have all seats in the upright position, trays stored, and seatbelts fastened." Flight attendants passed through the aisles checking. The aircraft could not leave the gate until everyone was locked in, and the two beside Tom were not.

The flight attendant noticed the situation and opened the last overhead bin. He pulled out two small straps with seat belt buckles. After a few adjustments, he used these to extend the seat belts on Tom's new close companions. For the entire flight, Tom did not move, no beverage, no snack, no toilet, no breathing.

CHAPTER NINE

Key West

Flight 401 landed at Miami International Airport at 1:24 p.m. The aircraft emptied before Tom's companions departed. He was the last to leave and was struggling down the aisle. His left leg had fallen asleep during the flight. The feeling in his leg did not return until he exited the aircraft. He continued the march up the gangway into the terminal.

Tom rented a car and drove the five hours to Key West. He looked at the passing scenery.

I don't remember this drive being this long. I don't mind it, but the traffic when I pass through one of the keys is a distraction. Especially Key Largo and Marathon, but these bridges are boring as hell. I can't take the speed limit of 45 to 55 mph. Why can't they build an expressway from Key Largo to Key West?

With the traffic, Tom did not pull into Key West until after 6 p.m. He started his search for a hotel. Beachfront hotels in Key West are costly. Not that Tom could not afford one, but he lived at the beach. *Why throw money away, water is water, is it not?* Smaller hotels and motels off the beach were not much cheaper, and many charged for parking or had none at all.

Nothing looked like it would suit Tom's pocketbook until he entered the south end of the Key. There he spotted a sign,

"Vacancy… Cheapest hotel rates in Key West." He pulled up to the modest motel. It had parking in front of the units — a good sign, indicating free parking.

There was a parking spot at the front office. Tom entered. A string bean of a youth, no older than sixteen with zits covering his sunburned hairless freckled face, greeted him. "Welcome to the Low Key Motel. What room can I show you, single or double?" giggled the teenager.

"Why aren't you in school? Don't they go to school in Key West?" Tom quizzed the startled motel clerk.

"I graduated last year and besides school's out at 3:30 p.m.," answered the clerk handing Tom a card from a holder on the counter.

"Is this you, Assistant General Manager? You must get promoted fast here in the Keys."

"Sure do, when your father owns the company."

Tom had a puzzled look as he surveyed the business card, "How do you pronounce your name?"

"Just like its spelled Harvey L-i-p-s-h-i-t-s, Lipshits, it's German." answered thirty-two gleaming extra-large white teeth. He just stood there in his open toe sandals with black socks, yellow and blue checked shorts and a tie-dyed t-shirt with frizzy red hair puffing out of his head.

Tom was staring. "Why the socks with the sandals?"

"I don't like sand in my toes. Feels scuzzy."

"Very well, Harvey. How much for a single?"

"One hundred seventy-five dollars," there were those smiling white teeth again.

"You gotta be kidding," answered a shocked Tom.

RED LIPS

"Nope, you're in the Keys. We don't come cheap," said the white teeth in the red face.

"I know some hookers that might release some of that head pressure of yours," answered Tom. He accepted the room key after he decided he needed some rest from this morning's flight.

Room 13 was a bit small, but it had a bathroom with a shower stall and a single bed. There was a suitcase stand for his luggage but no dresser. A twenty-one-inch TV hung from the wall. The front window, beside the bed, contained a small air-conditioner. The only other light beside the ceiling light was a reading lamp hung off the headboard. Tom would not be walking barefoot on the robin's egg blue shag carpet that looked speckled with new and old mysterious stains. If it weren't for the dirt on the walls, they would be bare.

Tom had lived in Key West before he found the sunken treasure, but that was over seven years ago. He wondered if everyone still hung out at Mallory Square to watch the sunset. He decided to check with Harvey at the reception desk.

"Well, it's almost sunset time, and everyone will be heading down to the water. There are many popular restaurants and bars to watch the sunset. But on your budget, I suggest Mallory Square at the end of Whitehead Street."

Tom shook his head and left. Luckily, the Low Key was only a few blocks from Whitehead, and Tom strolled down to the square. The crowd packed into Mallory Square. There was plenty to see, even before the sun set, with musicians, clowns, artists, and food vendors.

It was easy for Tom to mingle with the crowd. He did his handshakes and howdys, looking for some locals who might help with his search. Most did not live here or were not interested.

Suddenly, he was jostled by a young man who said, "Excuse me, sir." The accent was familiar, a New Yorker. He looked at the man's cap, and there was the orange N Y against the royal blue background. A New York Met's baseball fan. Another thing attracted Tom to this youngster, his dress. He was wearing a bright red shirt with a large fish on the left chest. Over the fish read, *YANKEE CAPTS CHARTERS, Key West, FL*. They struck up a conversation.

"So where in New York, are you from?" quizzed Tom.

"Long Island, how d'ya know?"

"Can't miss the accent. I'm from Jersey; the name's Tom Walker." Tom stretched out his hand.

The young man replied, "Michael Young," accepting the handshake.

Michael Young was twenty-four years old. He was about the same size as Tom, five feet eight. Much more muscular, but not weightlifter muscular. No, hardworking muscular. Those arms did heavy lifting for a living. He had a shaved head. The shaggy goatee on his chin replaced the missing hair on his head. A friendly smile sat in the middle of his tanned face.

"Michael, you look like you could use a drink?" and he reached over to one of the vendors and grabbed two beers.

They chugged both beers.

"Another?" Tom suggested.

"Sure, if you're buying," replied Mike wiping the foam off his face.

The conversation continued, "What are you doing in Key West?"

"I live here," replied Mike, "moved from Long Island about a year ago."

"Is your family here?"

"Nope, I came alone."

It was challenging to get Mike to spill everything about himself. But Tom thought this could lead to some valuable information. He decided another beer might help.

"How do you support yourself?"

"Fishing."

"Great, but I never heard of it paying well."

"Oh! Well, I work on a charter boat here. We take fishermen out for three or four days at a time. I do well," said Mike pointing to the shirt with the *YANKEE CAPT* logo. "Tips are fantastic."

"Gee, how did you snag that gig?" Tom was trying to keep the conversation going and using some of his hip jargon, or so he thought.

"I lived in Freeport, where the party fishing boats go out. My father took me on one when I was about twelve. There was a group of children like me, and I started helping them fish, baiting their hooks, and helping them bring in any fish they caught. I had been fishing since I was five years old with my father."

"Your father liked to fish?"

"Hell, yes. Dad's a clam digger on Long Island."

"So, your father got you a job on a fishing boat?"

"No. The captain of the party boat offered me a weekend job supervising groups of children. That was my passion. Helped with my expenses all through high school and college."

Mike took a swig of beer.

"When the crew down here needed another hand, one of the crewmen who had met me up north before recommended me. I came down for an interview and was working by the next weekend. Been here ever since." Mike pulled on his goatee. "The boat will be in drydock next month for repairs so I plan on going back north, make the rounds, know what I mean?"

"Sure, gotta show the folks you're still alive."

"Yeah, and what are you doing down here? You don't look like the typical tourist."

"I'm not, I'm looking for someone. Here look at this."

Tom pulled out the picture of Michael Summerfield and handed it to Mike.

"Ever see him around here?"

Mike studied the photo while scratching his goatee. "He looks kinda familiar."

"His boat was a forty-three-foot Carver coupe named the *Thumbs Up,* and he was here in April."

Mike's eyes lit up, "Yeah, I remember him now. Cool boat. He docked close to us at the marina. He was there for about a week. Seems to me he left after some argument with this lady."

"What lady?"

"I don't know. He'd left the boat to get supplies or something, and this woman came sneaking onto the boat. There was something strange about the way she was acting like she didn't want to be noticed. The guy came back. She came out of the cabin and kissed him. She stayed a night or two. They argued, shouting and all. I think she threw a bottle at him. I heard the crash. Anyway, she stormed off the boat, and he left."

RED LIPS

"What did she look like?"

"A million dollars, tall, black hair, straight. I walked by her once. She looked good, a little old but well put together. Her lips were full, and she wore this bright red lipstick that made them look perfect."

"Anything else?"

"Yeah, now that you mentioned it, she smelled good."

"Thanks, Mike, you've been a great help." He pulled a twenty-dollar bill out and handed it to Mike.

"Thanks, but I don't need this. Let me buy you one." He handed the money back to Tom and grabbed two beers from the vendor and laid an Andrew Jackson bill on the counter.

Mike finished his beer and deserted Tom after advising him of an early charter he had the next morning.

A stranger in the distance was staring at Tom. As Tom started towards the man, he noticed a scar across his right cheek. Before Tom could make contact, the man limped back into the crowd.

It had been a long day, and he decided to go down to the pier tomorrow and ask if anyone else had seen Michael Summerfield.

He meandered back to the Low Key Motel. Waiting for him was the one thing he needed most, a bed. He brushed his teeth, washed his face, flopped onto the mattress, and fell sound asleep.

The scarred man pulled a cell phone from his pocket. "Hi, Boss. Yeah, I got a tail on him. We're in the Keyes. Uh-huh, will do."

After a few minutes, he was beginning to dose off. Drip...drip...drip... something was wrong. Tom sat up in bed.

What's that, a leaking faucet? He darted into the bathroom to check, and, here was the sink faucet with the drip.

Tom attempted to tighten the handle. It just spun, *stripped.* He took the only face towel from the rack and placed it in the sink. *There. At least it's muffled.*

The next couple of hours were heavy. Tom slept soundly, but at two a.m., there was a ruckus outside the back window. The Low Key Motel abutted a youth hostel in the back. There, a menagerie of young men and women had decided to throw a party. They ended at three-thirty in the morning after some coaxing from Tom.

A quiet night's sleep was still not in Tom's forecast. At five-thirty sharp, the locals decided to celebrate the sunrise. "Cock-a-doodle-doo," they kept crowing.

Giving up, he rose and took a shower and shaved. Walking out of the motel, he continued down towards the pier.

There he found a small coffee shop just opening. It took three cups before he could get his mind back. Tom asked the waitress if she heard of the *Yankee Capt.* She gave him directions to its berth. That would be his next stop.

After retrieving his car, he drove to the pier. It was still early, and most of the boats were still there preparing for the day's fishing charters. One of the crews from another ship was storing supplies on board. Tom greeted him and queried if he had seen the *Thumbs Up.*

"Yes, it docked over there," said the fisherman pointing further down the dock.

"Did you talk to the captain at all?"

"Nope, we don't cotton to strangers down here unless we have to."

"I see," responded Tom.

"But he did seem friendly with the harbormaster. Might want to talk to him."

"Thanks, I think I will. Where can I find him?"

"See that white building at the end of the marina? The one with the blue metal roof?"

"Yes."

"Well, he's usually in there jawing with the old Cods 'bout this time of day."

"Old Cods?"

"Old fishermen. They congregate there every morning for coffee and fish stories."

"I see. Thanks for your help."

"Nice talk'n ta ya," said the fisherman as he returned to his chores.

It took about fifteen minutes for Tom to traverse the short distance to the white building as he stopped at every boat to question the men.

As he approached the white stucco building, he noticed there was no sign. Nothing indicated this was the harbormaster's office. He entered through the weathered red door into a single room with four men sitting at a rustic wooden table. A small counter with four stools stood at the far wall across from the café's door.

Tom ambled up to the counter.

"Can I help you?" asked the older grey-haired woman.

"Yes, coffee regular, please."

She poured the coffee into a white mug with a blue anchor embossed on it. On top of the anchor read, "No Name."

"That'll be two dollars."

Tom dropped two singles and a quarter on the counter. He proceeded to the table.

"Good morning. Do you mind if I join you, gentlemen?" asked Tom.

"Pull up a chair," answered the weathered man in the captain's cap.

"Thanks."

After adjusting to the chair, Tom asked, "Did any of you, by chance, talk to a Michael Summerfield? He was here a couple of weeks ago, with his yacht *Thumbs Up.*"

"Yes, I recall talking with Mr. Summerfield," answered the man with the cap.

"Mr. Summerfield was to arrive in Cancun last week but is missing. I am trying to locate him," explained Tom.

"I told that sand crab he was a fool to try to make the crossing in such a boat. Wouldn't listen. Insisted on going. Serves him right. I take that back. No man deserves to be swallowed by Davy Jones. How can I help?"

"Do you know the route he planned to take?"

"He didn't have a clue. Came from Newport. Kept bragging about America's Cup races in the '60s and '70s. That's not sailing. If you get in trouble, head west, gonna hit land sooner or later. But, put a man in a boat in the middle of the ocean trying to find a small dot of an island. Now there's a seadog of a sailor."

"What did you tell him?"

"The best way from here is to head west to Dry Tortugas. From there south to Cuba. Takes a lot of dead reckoning and course adjustments. Follow the coast sailing southwest until you get to the tip of Cuba. A place called Cabo San Antonio. Then the hard part, crossing the Caribbean currents to Mexico. He was to head southwest to the coast. If all went well, he would find Cozumel or Isla de Mujeres off the coast of Cancun."

Another patron suggested, "Could be somewhere out in the Atlantic, lost forever."

"Thank you, gentlemen. You have been a big help."

"Hope you find him. Good luck," answered the captain going back to his coffee and conversation.

The answers all confirmed what Tom already knew. Just then, Tom noticed the scarred man at the end of the pier. The man kept staring at Tom. A chill came over Tom's body. This was no coincidence. Tom turned away and left the area.

He decided it was time for some breakfast and found a small eatery called *The French Chef.* Tom sauntered into this little café with the dark purple walls and black and white tiled floor. He took a seat at a small, well-worn wooden table by the window. A breeze from the large white fans overhead gave a pleasant waft of air against the morning humidity.

Paintings on the wall by Monet, Cèzanne, and Toulouse-Lautrec caught Tom's eye. Soft music filtered through his ears. It started with a song, *La Mer* by Charles Trenet and continued with *La vie en rose* by Edith Piaf. It was 1940's Paris.

A dark-haired waitress dressed in a white ruffled shirt over a black skirt came over to the table.

"Bienvenue to *The French Chef,"* announced the young waitress with long black hair and a French accent.

"Merci," answered Tom, trying to impress the young woman.

"Is anyone joining you this morning?" she continued.

"Sorry. No, I'll be eating alone."

"No problem," she answered as she removed the extra place setting.

She returned with a small menu listing the breakfast dishes available.

"Our breakfast special for the day is a classic French fine herb omelet with fried potatoes, toast, and coffee."

"What's the difference between a French omelet and an American omelet."

"The French omelet is lighter with absolutely no charring, and it is rolled versus flipped over. If you've never had one, you are in for a treat."

"Then a French omelet it will be," he said, enjoying her company.

"Perfect. And coffee?"

"Please, as soon as possible."

"Of course, *merci,*" she answered as she left to retrieve a pot of coffee.

He had still not heard back from Suzanne. He decided to make a call.

"Gallery 21, this is Cas." Castle Rock was one of Tom's partners in the treasure hunt. Since then, he had considered him a good friend and someone he could trust.

"Hi Cas, It's Tom."

"Great to hear from you. How's life in the Riviera Maya?"

"I have no complaints. How's the art gallery doing?"

"Just great, but that's not why you called."

"No! I have a small problem and thought you could help."

"Sure, what gives?"

"I took on this assignment to locate a missing person and think I may have chewed more than I can swallow."

"Since when did you become a Private Detective?"

"I let my ego get to me. Anyway, she was a knockout."

"Who was?"

"The wife, I'm looking for her missing husband. I could not help myself, Cas. It was like someone else answered her questions, and before I knew it, I was hooked."

"Why you?"

"I don't know. Someone recommended me, and my ego took over. I'm having a hard time finding this guy. To make matters worse, I think someone's tailing me."

"I don't like the way this is playing out. She could have gotten a professional, but she hired you. And why would anyone want to be following you?"

"I don't know the answer to either. What do you think I should do? Should I call her back and admit I can't do it?"

"No, you would never do that... would you?"

"Probably not. Not in my genes."

"I didn't think so. Why don't you call Holly? She's living in Newport. I believe she also has a close friend who might be just what you need."

"Thanks, I will."

They ended the call.

He decided to confront Suzanne on being in Key West. *Who else could it be?*

The phone call to Suzanne went straight to voice mail. He left the standard response, "Call me back."

Meanwhile, he decided to try Holly. After two rings, "Hello."

"Holly? It's Tom."

"Holy shit... Sorry, how ya doin?" she answered, trying to mimic his New Jersey accent.

"As best as I can on five million dollars."

"Five? As I recall, it was 8.5 million each."

"Expenses, doll, expenses. *My Fortune* is now my fortune, at least a good part of it. Then there was the purchase of the dock condo in Puerto Aventuras." They both laughed.

"Fine, but then, why the call? You're not asking me for a stake or loan."

"I am looking for a Michael Summerfield. He lives in Newport. Suzanne Summerfield, his wife, hired me to locate him. He went missing between Key West and Cancun on his boat, the *Thumbs Up*. Something doesn't sit right with me. Can't place my finger on it. Could you check her out for me? Make sure she is legit."

"Sure, do you have an address?"

Tom gave Holly the address from the check. She promised to get back to him in a couple of days.

"Oh! One more thing. Cas said you could get me in touch with someone on a security matter." He explained about the scarred man following him.

"I have just the man. But he is very secretive of his identity. I'll call him and have him call you. He will identify himself as Moshe Kaplan."

"Moishe, that is a funny name."

"No Moshe as in mocha. Like Moshe Dayan, that famous Israeli military leader."

"Oh, yes, I remember him, but I thought you said he did not want anyone to know his identity?"

"I did not say that was his name."

"Oh! Thanks, I'll be waiting for his call," Tom disconnected.

There seemed to be nothing more to do in Key West. Tom dashed back to the motel and checked out. Harvey was there with his gleaming white teeth and a full set of gums, to thank Tom and ask him to, "Please come back soon."

Tom answered with a smile, "Sure." *That'll be the day.*

After turning in his rental and going through the short TSA checkpoint, Tom was once again at the gate for Aerolineas Uno Dos Tres. A quick survey of the lounge area revealed no one needing an extension for their seat belt. There was a family with a young boy, two teenage girls, and the usual business people and tourists. No one to worry about, thought Tom.

His cell vibrated in his pocket. After extracting it, he looked down. It was Suzanne returning his call.

"I have questions," began Tom's greeting.

"No, hello, how are you? Curt, aren't we?"

"Well, yes. Sorry about that, but I heard some disturbing news yesterday."

"And what was that?"

"You told me you last talked to your husband over the phone while he was in Key West."

"That's correct."

"Well, I have at least two people who saw you get on the *Thumbs Up.* They also noticed you had a loud argument with Michael. Beer bottles were smashed, and you stormed off. I can't help you if you're not telling me everything."

"Tom, calm down, I was never in Key West. I don't know who that woman was, but it wasn't me. I swear. Maybe, that woman is why he is missing."

"I hope you're telling me the absolute truth because I will find out."

"I have nothing to hide."

"There's one more thing."

"What's that, Tom?"

"You never made a missing person's report to the police."

"You're right. We must talk. You're upset. I'm flying down tomorrow. I'll call you when I settle in."

She disconnected the call before Tom could respond.

CHAPTER TEN

The Return

The boarding process had begun, and Tom located his seat, 36B, between the two teenage girls and in front of the couple with the young boy. Fifteen minutes later, they took off into the sky.

The girls started holding a conversation across Tom. It seemed that one girl was not happy about the way some other girl in Key West was looking at her, hopefully, soon-to-be boyfriend.

"Did you see the way Sharon made eyes at my Tommy," said the one on his left.

"Ya, she was after him alright," answered the girl on his right in between chewing her gum.

"Well, I'm disinviting her to my party. Am I right, Courtney, or am I wrong?"

"You're right, Stacy, you're right," said Courtney sticking another slice of gum in her mouth.

The pain Tom received from Johnny boy, seated behind him, interrupted this inspiring conversation. It seemed the six-year-old, worrying about getting blood clots over this long flight, decided to exercise his legs by kicking the seat in front of him, Tom's.

Thankfully, the flight landed fifteen minutes early. Unfortunately for Tom, no one was there to guide them into the arrival gate at that time, so they parked away from the terminal for those minutes.

Meanwhile, two wide-body aircraft came in from Britain and Canada with over 500 passengers. They crammed into the Customs and Immigration areas causing massive lines going out the door.

Aerolineas Uno Dos Tres pulled into their gate only to be told by Mexican officials that one of the widebody aircraft arrived late and caused the Immigration hall to be over crowded.

"Everyone must remain on board until I get permission to release passengers. I am sorry for the inconvenience," said the official.

After twenty minutes, the official released the aircraft. Passengers then made their way down a long corridor to an escalator. At the bottom roped off lines channeled the crowd through the hall towards the podiums along the back wall. The room was still full, and the passengers had to disperse themselves among the available openings.

Since Tom was a resident, he did not have to go in the tourist lines, which were again bulging out into the hallway. It took only ten minutes before Tom snaked his way through the resident line. After a brief conversation with the immigration officer, Tom had his passport stamped, and was free to pass.

Tom's next obstacle was the baggage carousels. With no checked baggage, he did not need to stop so continued to the Customs agents waiting at the exit.

There a line of travelers waited to press the button on the red and green lights. Tom watched as family after family pressed the button and received the green GO light. It was Tom's turn, and he proudly stepped up to the light and pressed, RED light *(meaning go directly to jail do not pass go)*.

The officer took him to the side and forced him to open his bag. This time he cleared with no problem. Next obstacle, marching through the gauntlet of timeshare hawkers waiting at the exit as they tried to snag unsuspecting tourists with offers of local information and transportation to their hotels.

Vacating the terminal, he approached the taxi stand and hired a taxi to transport him back to Puerto Aventuras. But not before he spotted the scarred stranger.

He turned away for a second, and the stranger disappeared. *Perhaps, I'm getting paranoid.* Besides, he was too exhausted to worry about that at the moment, and Holly had said this Moshe Kaplan would help with that situation.

CHAPTER ELEVEN

Puerto Aventuras

The next morning passed with no issues. Later, Tom strolled down to Manny's for a Corona. While staring into the gold brew, he reminisced about his life before accepting this challenge. Carefree, no one tailing him, no problems to solve except which bar to enjoy that night.

The vibration of his cell phone disrupted his thoughts. He scanned the incoming number and answered, "Hello."

"It's me. I'm at the Omni. Room 325. I'll be waiting."

No need for names he knew who it was. The silky voice. Her voice was the chum and her lips the bait. She'd casted the line and hooked the mark. Only this time, the prize was Tom Walker. He'd go. You bet he'd go.

It only took a few minutes to cross the marina and enter the Omni lobby. There was no need for the elevator. He sprang up the two flights to room 325.

Tom knocked on the door.

"It's open."

He opened the door, and there was Suzanne. She was spread out across the sofa wearing a man's white style shirt tied at the waist. Tom could picture her nipples through the shirt. Her red shorts barely covered her tight ass. And of course, there was the Chanel No. 5.

"Take a seat beside me, Tom," she said as she patted the sofa cushion.

Tom obeyed.

"Relax, Tommy; you looked all stressed out. Turn around."

Tom became aroused once again. He crossed his legs.

"Turn around," she said.

He did as ordered.

She put her hands on his shoulders. Her hands were soft, but there was strength in those fingers. The massage began to relax Tom.

"Where did you get this idea, I was in Key West?"

"Like I told you on the phone. Someone at the marina saw you sneak on the boat while Michael was out. When he returned, you fought and left in a huff."

"Wasn't me. No way. I was running a charity function that week. There were hundreds of people who will swear to it."

"What about the missing person's report? The police say you didn't file one."

"I headed to the police station to file the report. The desk officer did not seem interested. He kept saying, 'he'll turn up.' They said I had to wait at least a week. I believe they didn't want to jeopardize the tourist business with a possible drug issue. There had been something in the papers recently about a shooting at some local bar. But I insisted. He took the report, but I saw him slip it into his desk drawer. That's when I realized they were not going to do anything," explained Suzanne.

"There was nothing else I could do there. I got into my car and started driving. About an hour later, I calmed down and spotted a restaurant just outside of Playa Del Carmen. I pulled in for lunch. The place was empty so I sat at the bar," she continued.

"The bartender came over, and I ordered a martini. I was sipping my drink when I couldn't hold back the tears any longer, and I started to cry. Someone further down the bar came over and asked, 'Was there a problem?' I explained that Michael was missing. That's when your name came up."

"Sammy Sharp," interrupted Tom.

"Yes, that was his name, Sam Sharp. He said if anyone could find Michael, it was you."

"Very well, I'm sorry I got you upset. You should not have come down here."

"I'd do anything to help you find Michael."

"I understand. I'll find Michael, promise," said Tom. "Let me get back to locating him. I'll call when I hear something."

As he left the hotel, Tom made a beeline for Manny's.

Tom sat on his second Martini thinking, did he want to find Michael alive or hoped to console the grieving widow?

The conversation with Suzanne was still on his mind. She answered all his questions satisfactorily except one. Why me? "I may look the fool, but I am not," said Tom to no one.

"What was that?" asked Manny.

"Oh! Nothing just thinking out loud. I think it's time for me to go home," slurred Tom.

"Yeah, I think you're right. Don't fall off the stool. I'll put the bill on your tab."

"Thanks," said Tom as he stumbled out the door.

Tom was awakened the next morning by his cell phone, vibrating on the nightstand. He glanced at it, prepared to turn it off. It was from Holly. He took the call.

"Hello," he managed while still trying to get the juices back into his mouth.

"Good morning," a cheerful Holly replied.

"What's good about it?" Tom's morning crankiness had not left him yet.

"Come on, old man, it's eleven in the morning, and I bet you're still in bed."

"That would be correct."

"Get serious! I have the info you requested."

Suddenly, Tom came back into the moment.

"Great. Go on."

"Suzanne Summerfield is Michael's second wife. His first wife, Dorothy Bradford Summerfield, divorced him eight years ago. Old money, the family came over on the *Mayflower*. He has a daughter from the first marriage, named Marie Summerfield. She is seventeen years old, living with the mother but stays at her boarding school in Wellesley, Mass., during the school year."

"Why did they divorce?"

"He was having an affair with Suzanne. It was a very bitter separation from what I found."

"Michael must have a lot of money to cover the divorce and boarding school."

"Well, let me tell you. It looks like he is not as financially sound as he would like everyone to think. Dorothy got the house and a large settlement. He also pays for Marie's tuition, which is over fifty-eight thousand dollars a year. And, of course, Suzanne, with her spendthrift ways, has money flowing out like Niagara Falls."

"Do you know what Dorothy looks like?"

"Funny, not much different than Suzanne. I wonder why men seem to go back to the same woman they left."

"Yeah, me too. Well, that explains a lot. What about your friend?"

"He'll be calling you within the next couple of hours."

"What does this guy do?" asked Tom

"He'll protect you, and he is very resourceful in other ways. You'll find out. Let me know how it turns out."

"Will do."

Tom placed the phone back on the nightstand and tried to return to his sleep mode. He kept thinking about Dorothy. If she was the one who met with Michael in Key West, what was her reason? They were no longer friends, more likely adversaries. Perhaps it was Marie's tuition. Then a second call came through.

"Hello."

"Is this Tom Walker?"

"Speaking."

"Moshe Kaplan, I believe we have a similar acquaintance."

"Yes, we do. I've been waiting for your call."

"Holly tells me you have a shadow."

"A what?"

"Someone following you," explained Moshe.

"Yes."

"I was led to believe that money would be no issue."

"Well, that depends."

"Of course. My fee is $1000 a day plus expenses. Is that agreeable?"

"Is it negotiable?"

"Holly told me that's what you would say. No."

"What guarantee do I have?"

"If you are still alive at the end, you pay. If not, you don't."

"I guess that works. How soon can you start?"

"I've already started. I'll be there tomorrow around 7 p.m."

"How about today?"

"Sorry. Not possible," Moshe continued, "Holly said you had a place for me to stay. I want to stay close by."

"You can bunk with me on the *My Fortune*. I have an additional stateroom."

"Perfect, it will save you something on my expenses. What's your location?"

Tom gave Moshe directions to his boat slip in Puerto Aventuras.

"Thanks. See you tomorrow."

The call was disconnected. Tom wondered what he was getting into with this stranger. One thousand a day for protection seemed exorbitant to Tom. He could probably get someone local for ten bucks, besides he didn't even know his real name. Moshe sounded like mocha. What kind of name is that anyway? Maybe he's a rabbi. *Holly recommended him, and I trust her. Tomorrow I'll know if I made a mistake or not.*

CLASSIC FRENCH HERB OMELET
Start to finish 5 minutes

Serves 1

3 large eggs

Kosher salt and freshly ground white pepper, to taste

2 teaspoons finely chopped herbs (parsley, chives, chervil), plus more to sprinkle on top

1½ tablespoons unsalted butter

DIRECTIONS
1. In a small bowl, use a fork to whisk the eggs. Add salt and pepper to taste. Continue to whisk until homogenous (the whites are one with the yolks, and not too much air is incorporated). Whisk in the chopped herbs.

2. In a small 6 or 8-inch skillet, melt the butter over medium heat and immediately add the eggs. Continuously stir with a heatproof rubber spatula in one hand, while moving the skillet around with the other hand. Occasionally swipe the outer edges and bring them in until you have small and creamy curds, about 1½ minutes. Remove from the heat and let sit 10 to 20 seconds.

3. Start to roll the omelet by lifting the pan's handle, tilting the pan downward and away from you. Run the rubber spatula underneath the top edge of the egg, nudging it to roll it downward until it reaches the bottom of the skillet.

4. Slide a plate under the skillet and tip the skillet, so the omelet gently falls onto the plate, seam-side down, and pointed at each end. Garnish with a pinch of herbs and serve.

The omelet should be fluffy and pale yellow. It takes a couple of tries to get this technique perfected, but the texture and flavor will reward you.

CHAPTER TWELVE

Moshe

The Omni Puerto Aventuras Beach Resort lobby was empty as Tom walked up to the front desk. A tall thin man in his thirties wearing a black suit looked up from the computer. "Hey, Tom, what's up?"

"Good morning, Gerry. Do you have any of those little bags you give to guests who arrive without their luggage?"

"You mean the toiletry tote, with the toothbrush, sewing kit, comb, shampoo, and such?"

"Yeah, that's the one."

"Which one? We have two."

"Two?"

"Yes. One for guests whose suitcase was lost by the airlines and one for the couple walking in off the street."

"What's the difference?"

"The second has a condom," said Gerry smiling.

"Of course. You got me. Skip the condom."

Gerry handed Tom two clear plastic bags containing small containers of toothpaste, shampoo, soap, a toothbrush, and a comb. "What's it for?"

"I have company staying with me. By the way, I heard you were going back to the States soon?"

"No, I extended my rotation for another tour. Three more years of living in paradise on the company dime."

"Must be great being an expatriate," said Tom as he waved goodbye.

"See you at Manny's," answered Gerry.

Walker never noticed the scar-faced man with the limp following him as he left the Omni, but a reflection that flashed in a window gave him the chills. He took note of the tall, heavyset gentleman with tattoos on his arms and neck — the kind of man who would call a dark alley home.

Back at the *My Fortune,* Tom made up the room. The bed only had a comforter for looks as no one slept there. The sheets and pillowcases were still in their plastic packaging. Tom made the bed and dusted the furniture. It would do for a couple of nights. *I hope this guy doesn't expect the Ritz,* thought Tom.

He was out on the deck, enjoying his first scotch of the evening when Moshe Kaplan appeared at seven. Dark, tan, well over six feet tall, all muscle and short curly black hair, he looked like he could handle himself and a few others. Standing there in light tan slacks, tan slip-on polished loafers, and a starched blue dress shirt hanging outside his pants, he approached Tom.

"Mr. Walker?"

"Yes," Tom replied.

"Moshe Kaplan."

They proceeded into the cabin, and Tom showed Moshe his stateroom. The one with the queen size bed. A quick scan and

RED LIPS

Moshe nodded his approval. After leaving his duffle bag, they settled in the lounge to discuss the events of the past week. Tom explained that Michael Summerfield had developed a combustion engine that ran on mostly water and had gone missing. His job was to find Michael for his wife, Suzanne. He told Moshe about the two men, Scarface and Tattoo, following him.

Tom said, "It disturbs me. I mean, why would anyone want to follow me, unless they meant to rob me. But these two made no attempt. They had plenty of chances. It doesn't make any sense."

"Of course, it does. Many corporations would consider this a disaster if it were true. Not to mention OPEC, who might consider this an act of war. I'm surprised you only have one person following you."

"No, two. I think I saw another one today."

"Well, there are reports of others who have developed similar mechanisms, who came to an untimely or questionable end."

"Like who?" Tom's face turned pale.

"Tom Ogle, who reportedly developed a carburetor that got one hundred miles per gallon of gas in a 1970 Ford Galaxy with a 427 cubic inch engine in 1978. He died in 1982, at twenty-four years of age."

Moshe grabbed a pot of coffee on the counter.

"Do you mind?"

"Help yourself," Tom replied.

After pouring a cup of black coffee, he continued.

"Stanley Allen Meyer, in 1989, invented a means of running the car solely on water. He died in 1998 of a brain aneurysm while at a meeting in Belgium with two financial backers. Neither of these projects was ever developed."

"But why are they after me?"

"They aren't. They're following you to the prize."

"What prize?" Tom stood and threw his hands in the air.

"Summerfield. He's the target," said Moshe. "Sit back down. You're making me nervous."

"What can we do?"

"Don't worry about people following you. That's my job. I'll handle it. Besides, if we see them following you, we know you're safe. It's when we don't see them, it's time to worry."

"Oh yeah, now I feel safe. As safe as a fly in a spider's web."

Moshe just smiled. One of the few times he would.

"Here's what I want you to do. Don't look at the guy with the scar. I don't want him to know you're on to him. But discreetly check all reflections in any mirrors or windows for his presence. Again, don't stare into the window too long, or he'll know what you are doing."

"Understood, I'll try. I'm sorry, you must be hungry. Would you like something to eat?"

"No, thanks. I'm exhausted after the long trip."

"I thought you came from the US?"

Moshe got up and placed the coffee cup in the sink.

"No, the Middle East. Let's talk some more in the morning."

The evening ended.

Scarface reported in, "Boss, we have a problem... A stranger. He just arrived... Yeah looks like he's staying... No, not an old friend. Younger, much younger... Sure, I'll let you know if anything happens."

RED LIPS

The following morning Tom awoke at seven, unusually early for him. Moshe was already sitting at the galley table with a hot cup of strong black coffee checking his cell phone, the four fingers of his right hand clawing at his cheek. Tom poured himself one and added some powdered milk and sugar.

"Isn't it a bit early to be calling people on the phone?" observed Tom.

"Where I am calling, it's the middle of the day."

He turned off the cell and stared at Tom for a moment.

"Why you? You don't seem the type of person I would think of hiring to locate a missing person. Didn't it seem strange to you?" asked Moshe.

"Yes. I thought so, too, and said so. Suzanne said someone recommended me. Perhaps I should have refused, but my ego got the best of me. She looked good, and I wanted to see her again. I don't get that many opportunities at my age." Tom smiled, "Now it's a matter of pride."

"I understand, but we need to keep this in mind. There is a reason Suzanne picked you that she's not telling."

Moshe stood up and started looking around the cabin.

"What are you looking for?"

"Charts."

Tom took Moshe to the chart table and opened an extremely wide drawer. Moshe shuffled through the charts. There were NOAA charts from Georgia down to Panama, including the Gulf of Mexico and the Caribbean.

"This is an extensive collection. I think more than you need," said Moshe.

"I had a charter company in Florida, both in West Palm Beach and Key West. That's where I met Holly. I guess you know about what happened up there?"

"No, I don't. Holly just told me you found a treasure."

"Yeah, but we almost died. I had some problems with some mafia people, and they found me just as we were diving for the treasure. We were lucky there was an FBI undercover agent on board. Between him and Cas, they saved our lives."

"Did you catch them all?"

"Not all. One got away, Joey Christos. But the last I heard he was in jail."

"Well, I'm glad you're all alive, especially Holly."

"So that explains those charts up to here. For the others I had an idea of perhaps navigating the canal when I got bored."

"So, you didn't take this assignment for the money?"

"No, it was her red lips that got me." They both laughed.

"I guess Holly's got me," Moshe added.

Looking over the charts, Moshe drew a line between Key West and Cancun, the projected path of the *Thumbs Up*.

"That's not the direction he took. The preferred route from the Keys is west to Dry Tortugas first. You then head south to Cuba and follow the coast to the tip, a place called Cabo de Antonio. Only then would you cross to Cancun. It is a treacherous crossing. This channel is the point where the Gulf of Mexico meets the Caribbean Sea.

"Was there a distress call from the *Thumbs Up*?" Moshe asked.

"No, I checked. There was no call at all." Tom continued, "So I believe there are two possibilities. One that the radio broke down and he couldn't send a mayday call and the other, the boat blew up and sank. If he went down with the boat, we'd never find him."

"There's one more possibility. Michael just decided to get lost and is hiding somewhere," offered Moshe, "So first we eliminate the sinking and he drowned with the ship, as that's a lost cause."

Tom nodded in agreement.

"Next, we eliminate, for the time being, the third option. If he decided to hide, it opens up too many possibilities."

Once again, Tom agreed.

"So, then, let's focus on the possibility that the vessel was somehow disabled, his communication system not functioning, or he didn't have time to use it and drifted off course." Moshe laid out the charts for the areas between Key West and Cancun on the chart table.

"If he was drifting, he could be anywhere along the coast of the Gulf of Mexico. Possibly the Florida panhandle, or Texas even. The prevailing winds are flowing east to west. You agree Moshe?"

"Perhaps. It would depend on where he was when he lost power and started drifting. There is a loop current in this precise area between Key West and Cancun that could take him further out to sea."

Tom ran his fingers through his hair, "you lost me."

"There is a current unique to this area," Moshe explained, "it runs from the corridor between Cuba and the Yucatan Peninsula north and then loops back out between Key West and Cuba and meets up with the Gulf Stream. It then continues up the coast past Bermuda."

"Man, I never knew that. How do you know that?"

"In my business, you need to know everything."

"Your business? I thought you were a bodyguard."

"Let's leave it at that."

They decided to break and continue the conversation over lunch at Papacito's. Moshe rolled up the Gulf of Mexico chart.

Moshe sat at an outside table overlooking the dolphin pens. Tom plopped into a chair beside him. A few moments later, Manny came by and placed sets of eating utensils wrapped up in a napkin in front of them.

"Good morning Mr. Walker, what brings you out from your abode on such a nice day?"

"Manny, I'd like you to meet Moshe Kaplan. Moshe, this is my good friend Manuel Sanchez."

"*Buenas tardes*, Mr. Sanchez, *como estas*?" Moshe greeted Manny.

"I'm fine, but my Spanish is not as good as yours. I was born and reared in the United States. How did you learn to speak Spanish without an accent?"

"I've lived for many years in South America, especially in Nicaragua, Panama, and Columbia."

Manny got out his notepad. "What will you gentlemen be having this afternoon?"

Tom ordered his usual chicken quesadilla and a Corona beer with lime.

Moshe responded, "It's too early for lunch for me. Manny, could it be possible for you to make me some huevos rancheros?"

"It's not on the menu, but it's my favorite, so I have the makings. You got it."

"And I'll just have black coffee with that."

"You got it." Manny took his leave and returned with the Corona and coffee.

Tom was checking out the dolphins when he noticed Scarface.

"There's Scarface again," he stated as he wiped the sweat from his forehead.

Moshe just smiled.

"I know you said, 'Don't worry about him,' but he still makes me nervous," said Tom.

"Focus on the task at hand. If the *Thumb's Up* were docked anywhere, we'd have located it by now."

Scarface's cell phone rang, "Yeah Boss, what's up?... Yeah, he's still here... They're having lunch at a restaurant... Can't, my battery is going dead. I'll call you in the morning."

"What about Cuba? You said that it was close," said Tom taking a swig of his beer.

"I checked," replied Moshe.

"How?"

Moshe put his cup down, "There are diplomatic channels. It's not there."

"So, what now?"

"We need to find Michael."

"How?"

"Last night, I thought of several other routes he could take from Key West to Cancun. Since he was not going by sail, he could set his compass for a GPS setting of N 21⁰ 16' 29" by W 86⁰ 45' 09".

That would only be 330 nautical miles and put him at the northern tip of Isla Mujeres."

Moshe laid out the chart across the table.

"The harbormaster in Key West advised him to use the route we discussed last night. This way, other sailing vessels would be in a position to help if he needed it."

"Understood. But how did you get your boat here?"

"I didn't need to. It was here when I bought it."

Their food arrived. Tom kept looking over his shoulder for someone or something.

"What's the problem, Tom? You look fidgety," asked Manny.

"Beverly," answered Tom.

"You're safe. Too early in the day for cougars to be out."

"Thanks, Manny." Tom relaxed.

Tom had just started on his meal when Moshe pointed to his knife and fork, which Tom used to cut his quesadilla into bite-size pieces.

"That's not how you eat a quesadilla. Just cut it into triangles and pick it up with your fingers," said an observant Moshe.

"I don't eat food with my hands, even fried chicken. It's an idiosyncrasy I've had since childhood. Can't help it," was Tom's response.

Moshe gave up and dove into the huevos rancheros. For the rest of the afternoon, they relaxed and watched the dolphin show. Scarface was around for the entire time. They made a point of not noticing him. Tom was starting to get a buzz, so they left and stumbled back to the *My Fortune*. While Tom took a nap, Moshe made some calls. One was to Holly. One was local.

Tom awoke to Moshe packing.

"What's going on?"

"I made some phone calls and have some people checking around for Michael. If he's alive, the only place I believe he could be is in Cuba. Possibly in a Cuban jail as a spy from the United States. They tend to keep it quiet until they can use it as a bargaining chip. Meanwhile, there's nothing I can do here, so I'm going to visit Holly for a few days and think."

"You're leaving me alone with Scarface? Why do you need to see Holly?" questioned an anxious Tom.

"If you can't figure that one out, you really are old."

"What am I supposed to do about Scarface?"

"Nothing. Let him follow you around, but don't let on, you know."

"And the other?"

"What other?"

"Tattoo. You know that guy with the tattoo."

"Same thing."

"While you're gone, I think I'll take a trip to Cabo San Antonio and ask around," said Tom, as he spread the chart out on the table.

Moshe looked down at the chart.

"Cuba? Tom, do you think that's a good idea? You could be taken as a spy."

"No problem, I have connections too. Well, money. I'll spread some around and see what I can find."

"Yeah, but can this yacht make it?"

"Yes, I've checked it out before. My fuel tank holds 1057 gallons of diesel fuel, and if I take an additional four fifty-gallon drums, I'll have plenty and some to spare for a round trip.

Moshe took a seat at the table and scanned the chart. He looked up at Tom and said, "How long will you be away?"

"I figure it should take me no more than two days there and back. One day to investigate. Oh, three days, four at most."

"Do you have a satellite phone on this thing?" said Moshe waving his hand around the room.

"Oh yeah. I went for the big bucks on this baby. If they had it, I wanted it. The dish is on top of the bridge. I can communicate from anywhere on the planet. At least, that's what the salesman told me when I ordered the yacht."

"Keep out of trouble. I don't want to go looking for you too."

Moshe grabbed his duffle bag and started for the waiting taxi.

"Thanks. I will. Give my regards to Holly," Tom yelled out.

"I hope to do more than that," Moshe yelled back, smiling.

Scarface reported, "Morning Boss. The new guy left... Yeah, I'll keep an eye out."

RED LIPS

HUEVOS RANCHEROS
Start to finish: 10 minutes
Serves 1

2 large eggs
2 corn tortillas
refried beans homemade or store-bought, heated
4 tablespoons Mexican tomato sauce
salsa
kosher salt and pepper to taste
queso fresco (or sour cream) and cilantro to garnish

DIRECTIONS
1. Lightly fry the tortillas, and pat dry. Put on a plate.
2. Warm up the refried beans and spread onto the tortillas.
3. Fry two sunny-side-up eggs (or once over if you prefer) and put on top of the tortilla and beans.
4. Top with Mexican tomato sauce, salsa, queso fresco, and fresh cilantro.
5. Serve with a side of fried potatoes and onions and sliced avocado if you chose.

CHAPTER THIRTEEN

The Trip

Back in his cabin, Tom once again pulled out his charts. He laid them across the chart table and charted his course to Cabo San Antonio. The current should steer him directly across to Cabo if Tom charted a course directly east. The battery was fully charged. All the equipment checked out, radar, sonar. A flare gun, fire extinguisher, and life preservers were operational. The only thing left was to fill up the gas tank. He would do that first thing in the morning.

He made a list of some emergency provisions in case the Cuban food did not agree with his stomach. A short trip to Playa del Carmen would be the remedy. The taxi dropped him off at Costco. He would renew his expired card at checkout.

While he was checking his shopping list and picking up the toiletries, extra batteries, and food supplies, he partook in what Tom called the grand buffet. At the end of each aisle was a station serving a taste of some sample dishes of pasta, cheese, cookies, or coffee. There were many items to try, and one could complete a meal on each visit. He was at the coffee station sampling some French Vanilla coffee when someone pinched his ass.

"What the…" Tom yelled out as he turned.

"Hi, Tom. Fancy seeing you here," said Beverly Mount.

"What do you think you're doing, Beverly? I almost spilled my coffee on my pants."

"Just checking out your tight bump," she said. "What's all this for?"

"I am taking a short trip with my boat."

"Oh! You finally have a client?"

"Yes. Now, if you'll excuse me, I have to check out."

"Me too. How'd you get here?"

"Taxi," answered Tom.

"I have my car, why don't we ride together? Save you some money, honey," offered Bev.

Tom agreed, and they walked over to check out. Hearing that Tom's card had expired, Beverly offered to put it on her Costco card. Tom accepted and suggested they have a hot dog and beverage before leaving.

Beverly found a table while Tom picked up the two dogs and two diet cokes.

"I tried calling you last night, but your number was unlisted," said Beverly.

"That's true."

"Then I walked by your boat, but you weren't there. I looked at your sign, thinking it would have your number, but it didn't. It just said Captain Tom Walker Charters, by appointment only. Do you know there's no number to make an appointment?"

"Yes," answered Tom.

"But you won't get any customers that way."

"I know."

"You want it that way?"

"Yes."

Beverly rolled her eyes, "I don't get it."

"I'm too busy as it is," said Tom taking a sip of his coke.

"Busy, all I see is you hanging out at Manny's every night and passed out on the deck of your boat during the day."

"That's my job," answered Tom.

"You know, Tommy, we're not getting any younger."

"Tell me something I don't know, Bev."

"You need someone to take care of you, otherwise you're going to make yourself sick and die."

"We all have to die sometime."

"Well, we should make the most of the time we have left. I think we are right for each other." She began playing footsie.

Tom placed his hand on his knee, trying to stop his leg from shaking. It did not work.

"Whadda ya mean?" His eyebrows came together. His eye twitched.

"We could share your home and rent out my condo. You know share expenses. Like those millennials do. Friends with benefits, so to speak."

Tom spit out a piece of his frank. "I'll have to get back to you on that," he looked at his watch. "I think we should go."

At 5 a.m., Tom left the dock with the *My Fortune*. Before leaving the marina, he stopped at the fueling dock to top off his tank and fill the additional drums.

"Did you say, 'fill it up'?" asked a surprised Juan.

"Are you hard of hearing? Fill up the tank and these four drums."

RED LIPS

"You know we charge by the liter here in Mexico? Today, that's one dollar per liter or four dollars per gallon. This isn't going to be you handing me a hundred-dollar bill like usual. We're talking serious money here. You have at least a 1000- gallon tank in this albatross."

"Stop your squawking and just fill her up. I know, over $4000. Here's my credit card," said Tom as he handed Juan his Disney card.

Juan didn't say another word. He just filled the tank and the four drums as ordered.

With tanks full, Tom received his receipt. His hand shook as he signed the credit card slip indicating $4521.

He returned to the cabin and poured himself a shot of Irish whiskey.

Next stop, Cabo San Antonio. The sun was rising, sparse clouds on the horizon were streaked with red. Tom did not believe in the old sailors' omen, *red skies at night, sailor's delight, red skies at dawn, sailors be warned.*

Off he bounded on his adventure. Tom's first attempt to enter Cuba began. All seemed well. *My Fortune* was running straight and true to form. The seas cooperated, with swells less than one foot high. He could ask for nothing more.

A scan of his GPS indicated he was twenty nautical miles off the coast. Time for a Corona.

It felt good to be out on the open seas once again. Tom has been locked into his berth in Puerto for close to three years, only venturing out for the infrequent fishing charters. They had only been dailies, never overnights.

Tom was enjoying his beer and thinking about how he would approach the Cuban coastline. He was seated on the enclosed flying bridge in his leather captain's chair, the one with BOSS scrolled on the back. It didn't take long for his peace to be interrupted.

Whoop. Whoop. Tom fell out of his seat. Approaching the *My Fortune* were two military boats, one coming at him from either side. It was time to ease back on the throttle. He could not outrun the 123-foot Stenka class Soviet-built Cuban patrol boats, at least not the AK230 30 MM gun pointed at him. But Tom was still twenty nautical miles away from Cuba in international waters. The boats pulled alongside both sides of the *My Fortune*. Their entire crew looked down menacingly at Tom, their 12 MM machine guns staring him down.

"*En espera para ser abordado,*" was shouted from the loudspeaker on the Cuban boat.

"I am American. *Perdón, per no hablo Español,*" yelled Tom.

"Standby to be boarded," blared the loudspeaker as a launch lowered into the sea.

Tom retrieved his passport.

As the launch approached from the port side, three Cuban soldiers boarded the *My Fortune*.

"What are you doing in Cuban water? Where is your identification?" commanded the tall officer.

"I...I'm fishing in international waters," answered a shaken Tom, as he displayed his passport. The machine gun still pointed at him.

RED LIPS

"No. You are in Cuban waters. Our territory extends twenty-four miles from the coast. Let me see your papers before I take you back to Cuba as a spy," demanded the Cuban officer.

"This is a mistake. What is your name?" asked Tom trying to defuse the situation before it got nasty.

"I am Lieutenant Edwardo Espinosa of the Cuban Navy. There is no mistake. You do not have permission to be here."

"Look, perhaps I drifted off course. You came to my aid. This doesn't have to be an international incident with the United States and Cuban politicians involved. Here, take this and get you and your crew some cerveza, and I'll leave. No one will know I was ever here. Agreed?" said Tom as he turned over his passport with the hundred-dollar bill slipped between the pages.

It didn't take long for Tom to be strip-searched, nor for the spot on the front of his pants to appear. He was not going to talk his way out of this one. He just hoped he would get back alive.

The Lieutenant's radio came alive. "Lieutenant, what is taking you so long? Why is the man naked?"

"We suspect he is carrying drugs, Captain."

"Well, hurry, we cannot stay here. There are other vessels out there."

"Yes, Sir," answered the Lieutenant.

The men looked at Tom and pointed their guns at him.

The Lieutenant was holding Tom's wallet. "Mr. Walker, is it?"

"Yes," answered Tom.

"You have a choice. Either give us all your money or the drugs you are carrying."

"I don't have any drugs."

"You will in a minute if we don't get all the money, and we will take you in to custody to Havana."

"OK... OK, here it is. All I have," Tom handed over the five hundred dollars hidden in the seat cushion. But not the other cash in the fish cooler.

"Now, we will get our cerveza. You will leave our territory immediately. Understand Gringo?"

"Si," answered Tom. He bent over and pulled up his trousers.

The Cubans left Tom and returned to the patrol boat.

Tom did not take the time to dress. He just turned the key and skedaddled out of there as fast as he could. The Cubans were not far behind. *My Fortune* was thirty miles out before the patrol was out of sight.

My Fortune was four hours away from Cuba and another approximately two hours to Cancun before Tom calmed down. He threw his soiled clothes into the wash, changed into clean clothes, grabbed a beer, and sauntered out to the deck

The weather turned without warning. Lightning began to strike on all sides. The seas began to swell, and clouds rolled in. A drizzle began. Tom returned to his cabin.

The twenty-foot high waves forced Tom to adjust course. He pushed the throttle forward, using all the power the boat had to fight through the angry seas. *My Fortune* was pushed to her limit. Tom steered the bow directly into the wind toward the waves. *My Fortune* rode through the first trough, up the face of the wave and through the crest riding bow down into the next trough.

Another appeared even higher than the first. Once again, *My Fortune* took charge as the yacht rode up a new face and through the crest. The ride down was like a Coney Island roller coaster, the bow plowing into the surf before it reappeared. Water ran off the sides of the bow.

The exercise repeated wave after wave until the thirty-footer appeared. This would be the test. Tom did the calculation in his head. The same calculation he had done a hundred times. Sixty percent of the 57-foot length of the boat equals a catastrophic wave height at thirty-four feet. *This would be a close one.*

My Fortune was ready. Tom pushed the throttle forward. It was now or never. Into the trough. Up the face. *My Fortune* seemed stuck at the top of the crest. Tom's heart sank as he heard the propellers whirring as they pulled out of the seas. *This is it.*

Tom held tight to the wheel. Suddenly, he was on a roller coaster as *My Fortune* crested the wave and came roaring down its backside. It felt like they were falling straight down and would never come back up. The bow slammed into the sea. Tom thought he felt the aft section of the boat begin to roll over. His heart pounded rapidly. His breath quickened. *This is the end!* Then the aft end splashed back into the water. His heart slowed, and his breathing returned to normal, but he was sweating profusely.

Tom did a quick check of the damages. Some glasses had crashed to the floor. A faulty cabinet lock Tom had on his repair list broke free. And a bottle of liquor left out on the table crashed to the floor. He could tell it was scotch from the smell.

He barely had time to get out the life vests. He grabbed one from under the bench. Before he got it on, a gust of wind blew the vessel on its side, ripping apart the tarp covering the extra fuel barrels. The dinghy tied to the bow broke loose and smashed into the windshield. Tom was holding tight. One hand was on the steering wheel, the other on the vest.

The boat was listing almost sixty degrees, and Tom was hanging from the wheel. A moment later, it righted itself. Tom's hand slipped from the wheel as he fell to the deck.

He stood up and placed his life vest on and surveyed the damage.

As he looked out the cracked windshield, he noticed another rogue wave approaching. It took all of Tom's seamanship to navigate *My Fortune,* but she ran straight into the trough, continued, and forced her way up the face. Tom's sweaty hands could hardly hold the wheel steady and work the throttle at the same time. Breaking through the top crest, he guided the ship down the backside into the pit. Tom was still shaking when the *My Fortune* popped up and righted itself.

The seas calmed down. Tom let go of the steering wheel for the first time in twenty minutes. He took deep breaths and wiped his hands on his shirt. The shirt felt like it had just come out of the wash. He did not change this time.

After he was sure the seas would not erupt, a drink was due. Tom found a bottle of Johnny Walker Blue he had hidden for a special occasion. He poured himself a water glass full.

With the danger past, Tom had time to reflect. There were things he wanted to accomplish before he died. This experience made him realize life could end at any time. He had come close to death many times when he was a young man. But then he thought he would live forever. At this age, Tom felt his time was running out. As he sat there thinking how close to death he had come, Tom realized there were other things in life that he missed, like his children. *No, he had not seen or heard from them in over*

RED LIPS

twenty years. Let's see, Thomas, or Tommy Jr. as he liked to be called, must be thirty-two by now. A full-grown man. He was probably married with children. And Sally, let's see. She must be almost thirty-five. I could be a grandfather.

It had been a messy divorce. I had my scotch up. No compromise. I stuck to my guns foolishly. Was it all Helen's fault? Perhaps not. I did work long hours, but there were the children. They needed a comfortable home. The kids blamed me. They refused to see or talk to me. But that was twenty years ago. At twelve and fifteen, they could be swayed by their mother, but now, perhaps not. It was worth a try. When this was over, I'm going to find the time to be a real father. I'll contact them when I get back.

CHAPTER FOURTEEN

Logan International Airport

Holly Flynn was at the arrivals terminal in Boston, awaiting Moshe. Her red and green scotch plaid skirt matched her flaming red hair and Irish green eyes. A white peasant blouse drifted off her shoulders. She paced between luggage belts in anticipation of this first meeting in over a year with her lover, Moshe, who saved her brother, Jeff. Moshe, who proposed she join him in Tel Aviv. How she missed his presence, but she had another priority: her career.

A large crowd formed by the baggage carousels blocked Holly's view. She tried standing on tiptoes but still was unable to locate Moshe. Stepping on the edge of a carousel, she spotted him entering the baggage area. "Moshe," she yelled.

Moshe turned his head and saw Holly waving frantically. "Here, I'm here," she yelled.

Seeing Holly once again, his hormones took control. He forced his way through the crowd, dropped his bag, and lifted her in his arms. The smile on his face also revealed the year of missed opportunities. He wished she would have joined him back in Israel.

"Kiss me. Kiss me. Is this real, or is it a dream?" she whispered in Moshe's ear.

She kissed him on his cheeks and his forehead until she found his mouth. One more passionate kiss. Not quite the movie kiss but one that ignites. One that would make Bogart and Bacall proud.

He picked up his bag, and she wrapped her arm around his as they walked to Holly's red BMW M4 convertible. Holly popped the trunk, and Moshe threw in the duffle bag. He opened the door for Holly and ran around to the passenger side and slid into the ivory leather seat.

"New?" Moshe asked.

"Yes, this one gets better gas mileage than my last Beemer. I've been visiting the family frequently since we almost lost Jeff."

"I don't blame you. Family is important."

"Did you retire from the Mossad?" she asked.

"Yes, it was a hard decision."

"But I thought you loved working for Mossad."

"I did, but my family is Druze Arabs, and in today's Israel, that means second class citizens. My family has been pro-Israeli since the 1948 Arab-Israeli War. They fought for Israel in the Six-Day War. As a matter of fact, they have fought with Israel in every Arab-Israel war. Last year the Israeli Knesset enacted a law with constitutional weight designating Israel a Jewish state."

"Can't your people do something about it?"

"They tried, but they could not get it changed. I am not religious, but my family is, and they feel this is a slap in their face."

"But why is your family taking this so hard?"

"Because we are unique in the Arab communities of Israel for our loyalty to the state. Druze are subject to the military draft, like all Israeli's, but Arabs are not."

"What about your Jewish friends?"

"They agreed with me and hope to reverse it in the future. Until then, I still keep in touch with my colleagues and many friends in Mossad. Let's get off the subject. It's a downer for me. I came here to be with you. Where are we staying?"

"We have reservations at the Lenox for two nights," announced Holly.

"Great."

"How is it going in Mexico?" ask Holly as she started the car and pulled away from the curb.

"We have a snag. I have feelers out with my contacts along the Gulf Coast. But until we get a lead, we're stopped. If he sank, there is no way to locate him or the boat. I'm hoping he drifted to land, or someone picked him up."

"What about the people following Tom?"

"He's still there. But at least he's visible. I don't think Tom's their target."

"So, who is?"

"Michael Summerfield, he's got the prize: the engine," said Moshe as they pulled up to the Lenox hotel.

They entered through the elegant lobby with its gilded ceilings and marble floors covered by only slightly worn red and blue oriental rugs. After checking in, a porter offered to take them to their room. Moshe gracefully refused, picked up his duffle bag, and Holly's overnighter as they headed for the elevator.

RED LIPS

The faux fireplace gave the room a warm romantic presence as they entered the Judy Garland Suite. She felt his hands on her breast even before he touched her. Her lungs expanded as she dreamed of what was to come this night. He turned. Holly couldn't wait any longer.

Holly placed her arms around him and kissed him gently on the lips. She unbuttoned his shirt and unbuckled his pants while Moshe did the rest. Her blouse fell to the floor, revealing her pearl white breasts. No need to fumble with a bra, she wore none. Moshe slipped off her skirt, revealing her red thong. It fell to the floor as he slid his hands down her waist. They landed on the bed in a passionate embrace. Their lovemaking did not end until late into the night. The heat caused rain to cascade off their bodies. Exhausted, they descended into peaceful darkness.

They did not wake until noon. Moshe called room service and ordered breakfast. They both put on the plush white Egyptian cotton bathrobes that came with the room.

"I missed you so much. I was afraid you wouldn't have time to see me," said Holly.

"I haven't stopped thinking of you since I left you last year. Being on this side of the world, I couldn't stay away."

"Won't that put Tom in jeopardy?"

"I repeat, Tom is not the prize. They hope he will lead them to it. I want them to let their guard down."

"You're not working alone, are you?"

"Precious, you know me too well. By the way, to change the subject, how's school?"

"I graduate this year and already have an offer to be the assistant curator of the Isabella Stewart Gardner Museum in Boston."

"That's great. I'm so happy for you. But, not for me. I would still love you to come to Israel. The offer is forever."

"I know, but I must follow my dream."

The knock on the door interrupted their conversation. The special breakfast included champagne and roses. They toasted. "Here's looking at you, kid," said Moshe imitating Bogart in *Casablanca.*

After breakfast, Moshe fled into the bathroom. He returned showered and shaved with a towel wrapped around his waist.

Holly was still in her bathrobe, staring out the window.

He walked up behind her and wrapped his arms around her.

"A penny for your thoughts," he was still doing Bogart.

"I can't remember Bergman's reply. Was it, 'There're only worth a franc in Paris?'"

"Close enough," answered Moshe. "So, what were you thinking about?"

"Us," she continued, "What I missed without you. Why can't you stay here?" She turned toward Moshe.

"It is not safe for me outside of Israel. I have done many bad things. Some I regret, most I don't. People are always looking for me. I will not put the one person in the world I care about in danger."

"Do you have a lover in Israel?"

"No. Only you. I have not found anyone else," answered Moshe. "What about you? I'm sure you have no problem finding dates."

RED LIPS

"Dates, yes. But nothing serious. No lovers. I don't think there'll ever be anyone else but you."

He put his hands inside her robe and let it fall to the ground. He kissed away the tear in her eye. They fell onto the bed. Once again, they were passionately in each other's arms. Exhausted, Holly turned her back and tried to go back to sleep. Moshe stroked her back, outlining the birthmark on her shoulder.

"Does it bother you?" she asked.

"Of course not. It's part of you, and I love all of you. You are perfect to me and always will be. Besides, I have my scars," said Moshe pointing to two bullet holes on his chest and an old knife wound on his back. "And look at my bald spot on the top of my head. I'm not as young as you think."

Holly turned and faced Moshe. She reached up and pulled his head down and looked at the spot.

"It's so small. It'll be years before you need to worry. Are you that vain?"

"I guess I am a bit vain."

CHAPTER FIFTEEN

Newport

Moshe's cell phone vibrated. He moved to shut it off, but it was from Tom. He looked at Holly.

"Answer it," she whispered.

"Tom, what is it? I thought you headed for Cabo San Antonio?"

"Never made it. Sorry to bother you, but I just received a call from Suzanne."

"What did she say?"

"She received a ransom call from someone in Cuba," Tom answered.

"You're stuttering. Calm down and give me Suzanne's number. Call her and advise her I will be calling." Moshe paused, then continued, "I'm in Boston, but I can drive down before I leave and talk to her. I think we will get more information face to face than over the phone."

"Agreed." Tom gave Moshe the number. "I'll call her immediately," Tom said quickly.

"Stay calm. How is Scarface?"

"Still around," answered Tom.

"Good. See you in a day or two. I'll keep in touch."

The call ended.

After giving Tom some time to contact Suzanne, Moshe made the call.

"Hello."

"Hello. Is this Suzanne Summerfield?"

"Speaking, and who is calling?"

"Moshe Kaplan, I believe Mr. Walker advised you I would be calling."

"Yes, he did. How can I help you, Mr. Kaplan?"

"I'm here in Boston and would like to meet with you tonight to go over what we know so far and see if there is anything you could add to it."

"I would love to, but unfortunately, I have a meeting tonight. Could we make it sometime late morning tomorrow?"

"Ah, I don't think that would be possible for me. I have an early flight tomorrow."

"Well, if you insist. I could be available after ten this evening."

"Thank you. That's so kind of you." Moshe frowned and shrugged his shoulders.

"Well, we have to make sacrifices to bring back Michael."

"Exactly," was all Moshe said as he raised an eyebrow and peeked at Holly.

"Do you have the address?" she responded.

"Yes, I believe so, 12 Ridge Road."

"Yes, that's correct. See you then."

She abruptly hung up.

"How did the call go?" questioned Holly as she started packing.

"Strange. I thought she would insist on meeting tonight, but she suggested tomorrow. I had to convince her we needed to meet tonight."

"Wasn't she frantic? I would be if my husband were being held for ransom."

"No, she was calm. Too calm."

They arrived in Newport after dark and located Suzanne Summerfield's home. Not quite a mansion, but close. The three-story stucco colonial stood at the end of a cul-de-sac. A graveled driveway passed through a porte-cochere leading to a three-car garage located in the rear. They parked under the porte-cochere and walked up the five fieldstone steps.

Suzanne met them before they had a chance to knock and escorted them into the living room. An elaborate crystal chandelier hung over a large marble coffee table. She offered tea or coffee, but Holly and Moshe graciously declined.

Holly noticed the large painting on the wall of a red kiss. Red kisses scattered around the house. Holly thought... *This woman has a kiss fetish.*

After the introductions, Moshe started the questioning.

"Suzanne, can you repeat word for word what they said on the call?"

"Yes, I think so. At least as much as I can remember, 'This is Generalissimo Alfonso Franco of the Cuban resistance group Alpha 66. We have your husband, Michael. He is safe, and he is being protected from the corrupt Castro regime. Of course, there is a fee for this service. The fee is one million US dollars. I will give you forty-eight hours to get the money. We will then call with the payment arrangements.' He hung up before I could say another word."

"Do you have a million dollars available?" asked Moshe.

"No, of course not. I would have to sell my stock."

"Very well. I don't believe in paying a ransom but get the money together just in case. When they call again, tell them you need to talk to Michael before you go any further. We need to be sure he is alive and unhurt. If the kidnappers give you instructions, stall for time. You'll need the time to get to me so that we can plan our next move. I don't want you to commit to anything before we discuss it. I'll expect you to join Tom and me in Mexico."

"I can do that, but first I'll have to get the money together. And how would I get the one million dollars through customs."

"I can arrange that if needed. Which phone did they call on?"

"The house phone."

"Give them your cell," Moshe ordered.

"Why?" she asked.

"So, you don't have to be home waiting for his call."

"Oh, of course."

"Good, let me work on this," continued Moshe, "and you get the money together."

"Give me your cell number," Suzanne requested, "and I'll call you as soon as I am ready to leave or hear anything else."

"Excellent. I'll arrange a room at the Omni Resort for you."

Moshe pulled out a small notepad from his back pocket and wrote down his cell number. He handed it to Suzanne.

"Do you need a hankie?" asked Holly pulling a tissue out of her purse.

Suzanne took the tissue and wiped her eyes. "We fought just before he left. There were money problems. I begged him to sell the patent instead of going on that ridiculous trip. He stormed out of the house, and I never got to say 'I love you' before he left. We always left with a kiss."

"Don't worry, Moshe will get Michael back for you."

"Thank you."

"Before we leave, can I ask you an awkward question without offending you?" asked Holly.

"I can't answer that until you ask the question. But, go ahead and ask."

"What's with all the kisses?"

Suzanne smiled. "I had a small cosmetics company specializing in lipstick. Perhaps you've heard of it, Red Lipstick. The red kiss was my trademark."

"Of course, I've used that lipstick before. I should have known. How did you and Michael get together?"

"We met at a charity benefit. It was love at first sight."

"I would think you could negotiate a great deal for Michael's patent with your business experience."

"I could and tried, but Michael has no business sense. I had arrangements with several oil companies, but he refused even to meet them unless they signed a guarantee that they would build the engine. But of course, they refused, so it was a nonstarter."

"What about the auto companies?" continued Holly.

Suzanne stood up, walked over to the fireplace, and stared at a picture of Michael. "They were not interested. It was too costly to overhaul their factories. Besides, they are gearing up for electric cars. I'm afraid that's all I can tell you."

RED LIPS

Moshe and Holly rose from their seats and started for the front door. Suzanne followed.

As she opened the door, she said, "Thank you for your help."

Later in the car. "Who is Alpha 66? I've never heard of any resistance group in Cuba," inquired Holly.

"Alpha 66 is a resistance group working out of Miami. The number 66 is the number of members who started the organization. Alpha represents a new beginning. I am not aware of any activities in Cuba except for short attack and retreat paramilitary operations. But I think I'll call an old friend from my tour in Afghanistan and see if he can arrange a meeting in Miami on my way back to Cancun."

Moshe pulled out his cell phone and booked an early morning flight out of Newport to Miami.

"No flights tonight, I have one more night. How about your place?" asked a smiling Moshe.

Holly headed to her condo.

"Moshe, how did you hear about this group?"

"Back in my Mossad training, we studied covert tactics. One case study when Alpha 66 attempted an assassination of Castro in 1962. The group attempted to contact the CIA and join the forces in the Bay of Pigs invasion, but they were not trained or equipped at that time. After that fiasco, they devised a plan to sneak into Cuba and eliminate Castro. It was an excellent plan. Luis, the group leader, had a cousin in Havana working as a security guard at the Cuban State radio station. Castro had a planned broadcast for noon on May 12."

Moshe stopped.

"Why'd you stop."

"You don't want to hear this. It's just covert stuff. Very boring."

"Not to me. I need to know how it ended. Continue please," pleaded Holly gently stroking the side of his face with the back of her hand.

"Fine. But remember, you insisted."

"On May 10, Luis, and two other members, dressed in black with darkened faces, were set adrift in a small rubber raft off the coast of Cuba under cover of darkness. The seas were calm, and the clouds covered the light of the moon. They pulled into a hidden beach and buried the raft and spent the night at the cousin's cabin in the jungle."

"The next night, they snuck into Havana and headed for the radio station. Luis' cousin had left a back door ajar. After entering the building, Luis made his way to the studio. There he located a small desk with a microphone on it and the Cuban revolutionary flag behind it. A large photo of Castro hung on the opposite wall. Typical of Castro's ego."

Moshe stopped, "Are you sure you want me to continue?" taunted Moshe.

"Yes. Now stop fooling around."

"Well, he opened his satchel and removed a package containing a time bomb. Gingerly he duct-taped the explosive behind the draw under the desk. He attached a small timer to the explosive."

RED LIPS

"A moment later, someone was attempting to open the door. Luis took out his pistol and was preparing to eliminate the intruder."

'What are you looking for comrade?' He heard his cousin's voice outside the door."

"I'm checking all the rooms as I normally do?' The stranger answered."

"I've already checked that one. I was told to keep it locked. Fidel is making a speech this morning."

"Sorry," answered the other guard as he moved on to the next office."

"Luis continued to set the timer, 12:15, thinking that should do it."

"He safely left the building while the guards were making their rounds."

"So, what happened," quizzed Holly.

Moshe continued, "Everything went according to plan. They made their escape and hid at the shack by the beach. The three huddled around a radio they set up, listening to the broadcast."

"The speech started on time, with Castro being his usual boisterous self. Fidel continued the speech; 12:14, 12:15, 12:16, 12:17, 12:18… No explosion."

"What happened? What happened?" yelled Holly.

"They could not understand what went wrong. That night they were picked up by a small boat and taken back to Miami."

"The next day, Cuban radio announced there was a small electrical explosion at the station at 11:15 PM, in an empty studio with no injuries."

"Luis was on daylight savings time… Cuba was not."

Holly laughed, "You made that up."

"God's truth."

"So... why did you study this case?" Holly asked.

He smiled and said, "To learn what not to do."

A short while later, they entered the condo and were once more in each other's embrace by midnight. Moshe was not going to waste a minute. He did not know when he would have Holly in his arms again. Stripping off their clothes, they fell onto the bed. Moshe caressed Holly's breasts and continued down to her thighs. They continued exploring each other until they passed out from exhaustion.

When Holly woke, she read the note.

Precious,

I didn't have the heart to wake you. Although it was a hard decision. Please reconsider my offer. Come live with me in Israel.

On my way to Miami.

Loving you 'til never,

Moshe

CHAPTER SIXTEEN

Miami

Going through Newport Airport security was a breeze for Moshe at this time of the morning. First morning flights are always the most reliable. No worries about arrival delays as they arrive overnight. Moshe located an inconspicuous seat at his departure gate. He dialed a past contact in the CIA.

"Long here," Jon answered.

"Jon, it's Moshe, I need your help."

"Let me call you back in five minutes. I'm in a meeting."

A few minutes later, Moshe's cell vibrated.

"Moshe, what can I do for you?"

"I need information," asked Moshe getting up from his seat and huddling in an inconspicuous corner away from prying ears.

"Whatever you need. I owe you."

"You don't owe me anything," answered Moshe.

"Hell, you saved my life in Afghanistan."

"That was a long time ago. You've repaid me many times over," said Moshe.

"A debt like that can never be repaid. Go ahead, what is it?"

"What do you know about a group called Alpha 66?"

"A paramilitary group, supposedly, still fighting against the Castro regime in Cuba. They maintain a compound outside of Miami. We keep track of them. Had one of our men on the inside, but they haven't posed any threat to the US. They put on a show, but it's just a social club used to get away from their wives. Mostly they spend the nights smoking cigars, drinking, and playing cards. Why?" asked Jon.

"Well, it seems they have my client's husband in Cuba and are asking for a ransom to get him back. What can you tell me about them?"

"Alpha 66 started in 1960. They planned an assassination attempt on Fidel Castro in Havana in 1961, but it failed. A second attempt in Chile, ten years later, also failed."

"I know all about that. But what have they done since then?" asked Moshe.

"They became a part of a larger group linked to several bombings and assassinations in Miami during the 1970's. But no Alpha 66 members were convicted of these crimes," continued Jon.

"What groups."

"Omega Seven for one. They were started in 1974 by Edvardo Arocena in New Jersey."

Moshe decided not to leave anything to chance. "Could one of the other groups be responsible for my hostage situation?"

"I doubt that. Edvardo was arrested in 1984. The Cuban community in Miami requested presidential pardons from Bush through Obama to no avail. Besides, being a sick man over 75, he has no power left. All the rest of the group leaders are dead or in nursing homes."

"But I haven't heard or seen any terrorist activities by Cuban groups in years."

"That's true," continued Jon, "today only Alpha 66 exists, still operational, although not actively. But they were one of the most ruthless of the Cuban resistance groups working out of the US fighting the Castro regime. For decades they worked with the CIA carrying out terrorist attacks in Havana and assassination attempts against Castro."

"They still work with the CIA?"

"No. Antonio Veciana, one of the leaders of the group, went rogue. He published a book called, *Trained to Kill: The Inside Story of CIA Plots Against Castro, Kennedy, and Che.* In the book, he revealed he saw his CIA handler meeting with Lee Harvey Oswald shortly before Kennedy's assassination. As you can imagine, this put the CIA in a bad light."

"Then, you no longer have contact with them?"

"Not officially, but they still have many contacts in Cuba and have assisted us at times with information on an ad-hoc basis. Still, it doesn't sound right. They don't have anyone stationed in Cuba that we know of, and I don't think they would take a chance on having us as an enemy."

"Perhaps, I could talk to them and see what they know?" asked Moshe.

"Agreed. Their leader is a man called Gonzales. He's a character straight out of a 1930's movie. Dresses in camouflage fatigues. He considers himself a general. Let me see if I can contact them, and I'll call you back in a few hours."

"Thanks, Jon."

Jonathan Long arranged a meeting with the man named Gonzales. The meeting was set for the afternoon the next day.

Moshe drove along a route that advanced deep into the everglades. The road, infested with alligators and crocodiles, led to an open patch of land where armed guards greeted him at the gate. They were expecting him.

The area was completely fenced. It protected the group from the local inhabitants surrounding them. The barbed wire on top would be for the curious tourists. German shepherds patrolled an inner circle.

General Gonzales greeted him at the gate and had him park his car just inside the compound. As Moshe exited his car, his sunglasses fogged up. He took them off, but the glare from the hot sun made his eyes squint. The humid air almost took his breath away. It reminded him of his days in the Costa Rican jungle.

Gonzales invited Moshe to climb into his open camouflaged jeep and escorted him through the facility.

A series of low cinderblock buildings lined up on the right and left sides. Men in wrinkled camouflage fatigues raked the area around them. General Gonzales advised the buildings on their left were the men's barracks. Moshe looked down and noticed three cigarette butts on the ground.

"Is there a smoking area for the men?"

"Yes, on the other side of the barracks," answered Gonzales.

"Do the men live here full time?" questioned Moshe wiping the sweat off his forehead.

"No. These men all have other occupations outside of this. The guard walking the dog is a cigar roller at a cigar factory in Miami.

RED LIPS

Our volunteers spend four days a month here at the compound. With that schedule, we can cover seven days a week, twenty-four-hour shifts, mostly on weekends. Of course, we are constrained on holidays. But everyone does his share."

"How many men do you have?" Moshe asked.

"We have a total force of 150. On any weekend, we have approximately twenty to thirty staying here. The barracks sleep thirty-four in each." Gonzales pointed to the buildings.

"I thought you would have more men."

"Once we had over 250 men, but the new generation, they don't have the fire in them. To them, Cuba is a third world country. Not worth saving. Since they were born here in the US, they have no flame in their hearts. America has made them soft. They don't remember what Cuba was or what it could be again."

"How do you support this operation?"

"We have some benefactors, corporate sponsors, but mostly member dues. It is a struggle acquiring the needed funds nowadays. But let's move on."

"What are the buildings across from the barracks?" inquired Moshe.

"Oh. Those are the mess hall, an armory, and of course headquarters. Would you like to see the armory?"

"No. But I would like to see where your men eat," requested Moshe.

They entered the mess hall. Moshe shuffled a deck of playing cards he found on the table. "I love a good poker game. Don't you, General?"

"No. I don't gamble."

On the way out, Moshe noticed the empty beer cans in the garbage pail.

Gonzales continued the tour past a parade ground toward the back end of the compound. The American and Cuban flags flew side by side.

"This is where we prepare for our return to our country," said Gonzales. He then motioned with his arm for Moshe to exit the jeep.

The General grabbed Moshe's elbow and guided him to a spot to view his training operation. Moshe shrugged his arm away.

The facility had men practicing for an invasion of Cuba. They were all in camouflage fatigues, crawling along the grass, shooting at undamaged paper targets representing enemy soldiers.

Moshe did not want to tell Gonzales that his men would not get ten yards into Cuban territory.

"An impressive operation," Moshe lied.

"Thank you. We feel we must keep the spirit of a free Cuba alive."

"I didn't think you were operating in Cuba."

"We're not. We infiltrate from time to time, but we don't stay. We operate out of Miami and sometimes Puerto Rico. We are relatively small. Most of the other organizations have disbanded. A few of their members have joined ours. We are critically underfunded at this time. The Cuban community no longer feels the need to support us monetarily. It has been a challenge."

It was doubtful to Moshe that they infiltrated Cuba. But he let them believe in their cause.

RED LIPS

A bugle played in the distance, and Gonzales stopped and turned toward the flags. They watched as the flags lowered and listened to the sound of *Retreat* over a loudspeaker. Everything stopped as all faced the flag and saluted, except Moshe, who placed his right hand over his heart.

They started back to the mess hall. "Can you join us for dinner as my guest?" Gonzales asked.

"Thank you for the offer, but I must pass. It will be dark soon, and I don't want to be driving back at night. Besides, I have a flight to catch."

"Then we should get on with the reason for your visit," Gonzales turned to Moshe and asked, "So, how can I help you?"

"I have information that someone from your organization has taken a US citizen hostage and is demanding a ransom for their safe return."

"Impossible, we would never jeopardize our relations with the US that way. We have helped the CIA in many operations in Central America."

"The man gave his name as Alfonso Franco."

"Never heard of him."

"Then I can do what I need to do without your interference?"

"I repeat, he is not one of ours and probably just a Cuban gangster looking for some easy money. By the way, how much is the ransom?" inquired Gonzales.

"One million dollars."

"A great deal of money, although I would have asked for more."

"Perhaps, but there could be complications getting much more together. I think they want a fast transaction."

"Yes, you are probably right. I would be satisfied with a million at this point."

"Well, he'll find it won't be that easy. Thanks for your help."

"Let me use my sources to get some more information for you. Perhaps I can be of some assistance," offered Gonzales.

"Yes, that would be appreciated. Here is my cell number. Call me as soon as you get anything."

"My pleasure, amigo," replied the General. "You will be hearing from me soon."

Moshe headed straight to the airport. He felt uncomfortable around General Gonzales. The General was hiding something, and besides, he had not heard from Tom or Suzanne and was anxious to find out if there was anything new.

But first, he called Holly. He found a secluded spot.

"You left me. I felt like a two-bit hooker in a flophouse in Times Square. I looked for the money on the dresser, nothing. I searched the entire room for my money. Again nothing."

"You're right. I'm sorry," begged Moshe. "But you looked so peaceful. I couldn't wake you. I left a note."

"Yeah, so does the John when he leaves. At least that's what I've heard."

"Honey, what can I do to make it up to you?"

"I want to see you in my bedroom before you leave. You've got a severe spanking coming to you, mister."

Moshe laughed, "You got it. Promise."

"Fine, tell me what happened."

"The place is a sham. They wanted me to think of it as a military compound. But a military base would be pristine. This wasn't. People were raking around the barracks, but cigarette butts were on the ground. The grass needed mowing."

He paused while a stranger passed.

"Men were shooting at targets but couldn't hit any. Patrol dogs came up to me looking for treats. It's just a way to get away from their wives for a few days a month."

"So, tell me what was so important you had to leave me for a romp in the Florida Everglades?"

"The man does have contacts in Cuba. Maybe he can be of some help in getting Michael back in one piece."

"I see. Just be safe. I don't want you hurt. Hear me?"

"Yes, dear."

"Now, you're learning. Go, do your job. Remember, I love you," said Holly smiling through the phone.

"I love you too," answered Moshe, replacing the phone in his pocket.

CHAPTER SEVENTEEN

Playa del Carmen

*T*ime to kill. Let me rephrase that. I'm bored.
Playa del Carmen on a Saturday night is a happening place. All the locals join the tourists in the streets, parading in colorful outfits to celebrate the end of the week and look forward to the new beginning to come next week. Street vendors ply their specialties. The smells of tacos, tamales, churros, and elotes (grilled corn on a stick) entice the spectators.

Tom decided he would spend some quality time Saturday night in Playa del Carmen. The last time he was there for the nightly festivities was more than two years ago. With Moshe still away, Tom thought he would give Scarface and Tattoo something to do if they were still following, and he felt sure they were.

It was a short walk outside of the Puerto Aventuras Marina to highway 307, where he caught one of the many vans, called collectivos, which drove up and down the road. They travel between Tulum and Playa del Carmen seven days a week. It was the cheapest mode of transportation in the area if you were willing to walk to or from the towns.

He walked through the entrance arch to the highway and made his way to the collectivo stop. He was the only one waiting. The vans passed every ten minutes. Tom watched three pass him. They were too crowded to take any more passengers. Eventually, one stopped, Tom handed the driver three dollars.

He found the last seat available, next to a local from Tulum. Tom introduced himself, and the passenger smiled and gave his name as Juan. The man looked like he was wearing his Sunday best with a white straw hat, bright linen shirt, and freshly pressed pants.

"You look very festive," observed Tom.

"Si. We are going to a wedding," explained Juan.

"Your daughter's no doubt?" said Tom pointing to Juan's daughter.

"No, my niece. Why don't you join us? Everyone will be there with cervezas and vino. And there will be a big parade."

"Perhaps later."

They approached Playa and made their way through the narrow streets arriving at the collectivo depot about 4 p.m. The depot was just a corner where you could connect to the other vans going to Cancun. It was only four blocks from Quinta Avenida (5th Avenue) or just Quinta as the locals called it. Quinta is Playa's main tourist pedestrian street. Quinta ran parallel one block in from the beach, giving glimpses of the turquoise-colored ocean at every corner. There were no first, second, or third avenues in Playa, only 5th, 10th, 15th and so forth. Tom never found out why, although the street numbers, running north and south were consecutive digits.

Tom strolled down to the beach and his favorite beach bar, *Bad Boys*. He could always identify it by the flagpole in front with the pirate flag flying atop.

He took a seat at the end of the bar next to some tourists. Pedro, the bartender, strolled over.

"Hey, gringo, where you been?"

"Hola, Pedro. I've just been hanging around Puerto Aventuras. Doing my usual thing. What about you? Still married?"

"Si, but with three *niños* and a *niña*."

"Congratulations. One more and you'll have your basketball team. Maybe it's time to take a break. Maria must be worn out."

"Never, she loves me," answered Pedro smiling, proudly showing off his gold tooth.

"I'll have a bucket of Coronas, por favor. What time does the music start?"

"Same as always, 6 p.m."

Pedro returned with the beers. Tom relaxed, watching the ocean waves and the fishing boats passing by.

The band started playing classic American rock at a little after six.

The American tourists struck up a conversation with Tom. They kept talking about their fishing trip earlier in the day.

"Yeah, I had this sucker on my line for thirty minutes. Must have been at least 200 pounds. Would have had that fish if that stupid wetback Mex hadn't jerked the boat," said the tall one.

"Yeah, what did you expect from a beaner?" answered the short one.

"How about another round?" slurred the tall man.

"Yeah, if you can get that taco head's attention," answered Shorty.

Tom couldn't hold back any longer. "Do you guys know where you are? Now, I know where the term 'ugly American' comes from." Tom had enough of the obnoxious American duo. He paid the tab with his credit card and threw a double sawbuck on the bar as he left.

He was getting bored again and decided to walk down Quinta to check out the shops. Tom missed the old Playa, as the locals called it, with the little shops run by families. The new Playa was becoming full of large stores catering to the new money coming in. Stores with names like Boss, Under Armour, and Skechers replaced the old, more straightforward names, Silver Jewelry, T-Shirts, and Boots. Then you knew what they were selling; now, who knows?

When Tom had first found this small fishing village in the early nineties, there were no American businesses, no McDonald's, no Burger King. Oh, they had a TGI Friday's once, but it closed within a year. It always amazed Tom how the expatriates who moved here to get away from where they lived wanted to change it back to what they left.

All the tourists from around the world were out checking each other. Most of the tourists at this end of the Yucatan tended to be non-Americans. The Americans wanted the craziness of Cancun. Playa was too quiet for them. But this was how Tom liked it.

He loved talking to the Brits, the Canadians, and the Australians. Even better yet, listening to the Scandinavians from Sweden. He also learned a few words. But the best was when he was around the Germans. Tom was fluent in German, but he never let on. All the tourists had exciting stories to tell, and they were always offering to buy a round of drinks.

As he continued his stroll, he could hear sounds of the Mayan flute music. Further up, the music changed to the sounds of a Mariachi band. He loved the feel of it all.

A crowd had gathered at the seaside park, Parque Los Fundadores. They were watching the Papantla dancers climb up the thirty-meter pole. Once the five dancers reached the top of the pole, four tethered themselves to four spindles extending from the top and launched themselves into the air spinning their way to the ground. The fifth dancer remained on the top platform playing the flute and drum.

Under the thirty-meter bronze sculptured arch, with the two young girls clasping hands reaching for the sky at the top, were the Mayan Dancers. Dressed in traditional feathered costumes, they performed for a smaller crowd. A couple of German tourists bullied their way to the front. Tom moved on.

At the edge of the park, next to the small white stucco church named Nuestra Senora del Carmen, Tom plopped on a bench and viewed the entertainment.

Scarface pulled out his phone and hit speed dial. "Hello, Boss… Yeah, I found him. He's on a park bench… Na. I won't lose him."

"Captain Tom, Captain Tom," yelled out a small boy running up to him.

"Jesus, my boy. How you have grown," responded Tom.

"I missed you. Where have you been?"

"Staying in Puerto Aventuras. Too much excitement for an older man here in Playa. Where's your grandfather?"

RED LIPS

"Maria is bringing him."

Coming towards the bench, the little girl in her red and white cotton dress led the slouching older man with the guitar. They approached.

"Grandfather, it's Captain Tom," announced Jesus.

The blind man smiled.

"Hello, Diego, how have you been?"

"Hola amigo, still here, playing my guitar. I have my family. What more can one ask the Lord."

"You have it all, my friend."

"Captain Tom, let grandfather play something for you? Perhaps, *La Cucaracha*, or *Quantanamera*?" requested Jesus.

"You insult me with those Gringo choices, Jesus. You know what I want to hear."

"I was fooling with you. *La Mariachi Loco,* it is."

Diego started into a rousing Mariachi song. A group of passing Mariachi's joined in. A crowd formed. Everyone was clapping and dancing to the music.

In the end, Tom handed Maria two twenty-dollar bills.

This is for grandpa."

"Gracias, Captain Tom. Come back soon, por favor," said Maria, but not until she kissed him on the cheek.

"I will, Maria."

"Jesus, take Maria and grandpa for some gelato." Tom handed him a twenty.

Jesus and his party moved on to another tourist.

Tattoo called in, "Comrade. I found him… Yes, I will stay close."

He continued up Quinta past the shops. One of the owners yelled out, "Hey, mister, come into my shop. I got just what you need. Almost free."

Tom yelled back, "Not today, call me when it is free."

Another pedestrian came to him, offering Cuban cigars cheap. Tom knew better. They were local with fake wrappers. He stopped at one of the regular cigar stores and picked up two real Cubans and a box of Mexican cigars at the lower price before he started back.

It was dark when Tom neared the collectivo depot. But then he saw Scarface. He watched his reflection in the windows as he walked past the shops. The man still had a pronounced limp. Scarface had been on his mind for days. *What was he after?* Tom had enough. Time to find out. He started toward Scarface. Scarface turned and hobbled into one of the side streets. Tom followed.

As fast as Tom walked, he could not catch his prey. After a few lefts and rights, Scarface had gone down a dead-end alley.

Finally, Tom would be able to corner him and get some answers. As he approached, Scarface pulled out a knife. He started brandishing it toward Tom. Tom was not prepared for a knife fight, not this time, and turned.

Scarface became the stalker, a cat on the prowl, and Tom, his prey. Tom traversed down different streets, attempting to lose him. But, to no avail.

The limp did not keep this cat from running. Scarface was still close behind and getting closer by the minute.

RED LIPS

Tom looked left and right, searching for an escape route.

Can it get any worse?

Then he spotted Tattoo at the opposite end of the block.

What am I gonna do?

He lost his bearings and didn't know where he was in the dark narrow streets. Scarface and Tattoo had him in their crosshairs.

Tom was not about to go down. Not without a fight.

Searching for something to use against them, he found a metal garbage can cover. A broomstick was laying against the wall. These were his only defense.

He started banging the cover, hoping to get someone's attention, but no one came.

A few feet away, he saw a narrow passageway between two buildings. Tom slipped in there. At least in there, they could not surround him.

He would fight them one by one. Walker was a Jersey boy from the streets. At least that was what he believed. But Tom had not been in a street fight in over forty years.

Still, he would go down fighting until the end. Scarface disappeared, but there was Tattoo. This was it.

Then, he heard the sound. The shrill sound of a trumpet playing. It was coming from the other side of the alley.

He ran to the end and fell over the high pile of garbage and landed on Quinta. A wedding parade was passing by. The playing Mariachis were leading a procession.

Next was a young man leading a donkey. On the donkey was a lovely young woman no older than sixteen. She was attired in a white cotton dress with a white veil.

There was Juan and his family. Tom ran up and joined them.

The procession continued down Quinta until they passed the taxi stand at the end of Avenida Juarez.

Tom said goodbye to Juan and jumped into the first of the waiting taxis. He lost his two stalkers. In the cab, Tom wiped the sweat from his face. He took deep breaths, trying to lose the shakes. They did not leave him until he arrived back at *My Fortune.*

Scarface made a call. "Did you get the money?"

"Yes. But I don't want the money I want you back home," answered his wife.

"I know, but we need it for the kids."

"Can't you find something else? Something not dangerous."

"You know I've looked. It's been a year and nothing. No one wants an ex-con."

"What about me? I can find a job."

"And I watch the kids. What kind of husband would I be then?"

"I don't care. Just come home to me."

"Understood. I'm doing my last job, I promise. Let me go. I love you. Kiss the kids for me."

CHAPTER EIGHTEEN

MOSHE'S RETURN

MOshe's flight arrived back at Cancun in the afternoon on Monday. After fighting the timeshare hawkers, he snatched a taxi and headed for Puerto Aventuras.

It was a comfortable ride until they hit the traffic light in Playa del Carmen. There always seemed to be a bottleneck as cabs, buses and trucks attempted to crisscross their way off and onto Avenida Juarez, the main thoroughfare in and out of the city.

An anxious Tom Walker was lounging in his salon, making sucking sounds with a bottle of Corona while waiting to hear what had transpired with Suzanne.

Scarface called in, "Boss, he's back... I agree... Consider it done... Yeah, immediately."

Moshe tossed his duffle bag on the deck. Tom jumped up in surprise. But, not from the sound of the bag, but the bullet that smashed into his window.

"Stay down," yelled Moshe as he hit the deck.

Moshe pulled out his Beretta 71 pistol and scampered along the dock, looking for a target. Taking cover behind the dock storage units and between boats, he scoured the entire area. Finding no one, he returned to the *My Fortune*.

Tom was still shaking. "I thought you said not to worry about those guys following me. You said they weren't after me. Look, they just missed me by a hair."

"Calm down, Tom. That wasn't for you. That was for me. I was the target."

"I got to get this glass fixed. How am I going to explain this to my insurance company?" Tom started sweeping up the glass.

"You're in shock, Tom," said Moshe pouring a drink. "Here drink this. You'll feel better."

Tom obliged, grabbed the drink, and sat in the lounge. His hands were still shaking as he brought the glass to his lips.

"Why do you think you were the target?"

"Because they had all the time in the world to take you out. No, they were waiting for me. The thing that surprises me is how they could miss."

"You're joking," said Tom. "You think they missed on purpose?"

"I have lots of enemies. I've done many things I regretted in the past. Things I can't take back. Things I must live with. But those people don't miss. Usually, there would be a skilled assassin or multiple hitmen. This was only one shot. One man who could take his time to get the right shot. He would never miss. No, this was an amateur. Anyway, he's gone."

RED LIPS

"I thought you were going to call. I'm going crazy here," said Tom, still in shock.

"I'm starving. Let's go to Manny's, and I'll fill you in."

Tom finished cleaning up the broken glass and started for the door.

"Why are you limping?" asked Moshe.

"Oh, just fell over some garbage the other night."

"By the way, how's Scarface?"

"I haven't seen him all day. Should I be worried?" Tom decided not to tell Moshe about Saturday night's confrontation.

"No, not yet."

At Papacito's, Manny brought over two Coronas with limes.

Beverly Mount was at her corner table. She sauntered up to Tom.

"Hi, Tommy. Who's your good-looking friend?"

"Moshe, this is Beverly Mount. Beverly meet Moshe Kaplan. He's staying with me for a while."

"Hello Moshe, I hope you're enjoying our little piece of paradise. Let me know if there is anything, and I mean **anything** I can do to make your stay a little more pleasant," purred Beverly stretching out her hand with the palm facing downward.

Moshe gallantly took her hand in his, bent down, and kissed the back of her hand.

"It is a pleasure, Ms. Mount."

"Call me, Beverly."

"Of course, Beverly." corrected Moshe.

Just then, Manny took his cue and approached Tom and Moshe.

"Are we feasting tonight or just having a liquid dinner."

"Sorry, Beverly. Very nice to meet you, but if you'll excuse us, we'll order our dinner," commented Moshe.

Beverly took her leave and sashayed to her table, parading her wares.

"Moshe, what will you have tonight? I already know Captain Tom is having the chicken quesadilla."

"Let me check the menu."

"Sure," Manny handed Moshe a laminated menu sheet. "The specials are on the board over the bar."

"Thanks, give me a few minutes."

"I'll be back, as they say," Manny left.

A ringing interrupted their conversation. It was Moshe's cell.

"Hello, Mrs. Summerfield... Yes, Suzanne, of course... Good and you gave him your cell? Fine, see you then."

Moshe explained that Suzanne would be arriving tomorrow and staying at the Omni. They needed her to be near when the next call was received from Alfonso.

Manny returned, and Moshe ordered the Yucatan fish tacos.

They enjoyed their dinner in peace as Beverly found another prize, a tourist who had just walked in alone.

After they finished, Tom asked, "What are we going to do?"

"I think we'll be going to Cuba. I'm just not sure how or when yet. Be prepared to leave at a moment's notice."

YUCATAN FISH TACOS

Serves 4

Salsa

1/4 cup fresh lime juice (2 limes)

1/2 cup fresh orange juice (2 oranges)

1 small red onion, thinly sliced (about one cup)

½ habanero chile, seeded and minced (1 teaspoon)

1 teaspoon dried Mexican oregano

1 teaspoon kosher salt

1 ripe mango, cut into medium dice (1 cup)

Fish

1/4 teaspoon cumin seeds

20 black peppercorns

4 allspice berries

1/2 teaspoon dried Mexican oregano

1/8 teaspoon cayenne pepper

2 medium cloves garlic, minced

Kosher salt

1 tablespoon fresh orange juice

1 tablespoon fresh lime juice

1 tablespoon olive oil (more if needed)

1 ½ pounds mahi-mahi fillets about 1 inch thick

Additional items

Vegetable oil for grilling

12 6-inch corn tortillas

2 ripe avocados thinly sliced

LEONARD DI GREGORIO

PREPARATION

Salsa

Combine the first six ingredients into a medium bowl. Cover and refrigerate for about two hours. Add mango and stir mixture.

Fish marinate

Toast the cumin seeds, peppercorns, and allspice berries in an 8-inch skillet over medium-low heat, occasionally shaking, until fragrant and the cumin seeds are a shade darker, about two minutes. Grind in a spice grinder. Add the annatto seeds, oregano, cayenne, and grind to a fine powder. Transfer to a small bowl.

With the side of a chef's knife mash the garlic with 1/2 teaspoon salt into a paste. Add the paste, orange juice, lime juice, and olive oil to the spice mixture in a small bowl. Stir well until combined. Rub the marinade over the fish. Place the fish on a plate and refrigerate covered for 30 minutes or up to 2 hours.

Assembling the tacos

Set your grill on medium heat and oil the grate. Heat tortillas in a single layer turning once until soft with light grill marks. Make in small batches if necessary.

Brush both sides of the marinated fish with olive oil and season lightly with salt. Grill fish turning once or twice until cooked through. About 8 to 12 minutes.

RED LIPS

Transfer fish to cutting board and coarsely shred or chop (your preference). Place a portion on each tortilla and with a slotted spoon, top with the salsa. Garnish with slices of avocado and serve.

CHAPTER NINETEEN

SUZANNE'S RETURN

The following day, Suzanne arrived. Tom escorted her to the Omni Puerto Aventuras Beach Resort and checked her in. They walked to her first-floor room overlooking the pool and ocean. After she dropped off her suitcase, they wandered out of the hotel to the beach bar in the back. Suzanne took off her shoes, and they walked along the beach, finally settling in two blue canvas beach loungers by an umbrella.

"I don't understand why they built those jetties surrounding the beach here?" asked Suzanne, pointing to the small structures.

"We are facing directly east toward the open sea. The undertow is treacherous. They use small walls to protect the guests who are not used to swimming in the open ocean."

Moshe joined them, and they moved to the beach bar to discuss their plan of action and get an update on what had transpired. Suzanne had not heard from Franco since last night but acquired the one million dollars cash. It was in her wall safe at home.

Suzanne's cell rang. It was Franco.

"Do you have the money?" Franco demanded.

"Yes, but first, I need to talk to my husband."

"Not possible."

"Then, no money. I need to know Michael is alive and well."

Reluctantly Franco agreed. He went into the hut and handed Michael the cell phone.

"Suzanne, is that you? Thank God."

"Yes, Michael, it's me. Are you all right?"

He broke down in tears at the sound of her voice. "Yes, just get me out of here."

"We will. Just remember, I love you. Put Franco back on."

He handed the cell back to Franco.

"So, what do you want?" she asked.

"I want the million dollars. I will meet you off the coast of Cuba, forty-eight hours from now."

"Forty-eight hours from now?" repeated Suzanne.

Moshe waved his hands back and forth, indicating no. "Make it seventy-two hours," he whispered.

"The money is in a safe in the states, and I need twenty-four hours to get it into Mexico. Let's make the meeting in seventy-two hours," said Suzanne.

"No, forty-eight hours if you want to see your husband again."

"Seventy-two hours for the one million, and I'll add another 250 thousand dollars extra for the additional time."

Greed, the great negotiator, prompted Franco to reconsider.

"Agreed, seventy-two hours. I will give you the exact GPS location in two days."

"I'll be waiting for your call," advised Suzanne as the call ended.

"Now what?" Suzanne asked Moshe.

"I'll arrange for someone from the Israeli Embassy to pick up the money and transport it here in a diplomatic pouch. It will not be subject to any search."

Tom's eye's opened wide, "You can do that?"

"Yes," answered Moshe. He turned his attention to Suzanne, "Can I have the combination to the safe?"

"Of course, but the house is monitored by a security company. I've notified them I'd be out of the country for the next few days. They'll be monitoring the house twenty-four hours a day. You won't be able to get in."

Moshe smiled, "Yeah, right. My problem. Can I have the combo? It'll make it a little easier."

She wrote down the combination to the wall safe reluctantly.

"If you'll excuse me, there are arrangements to be made," said Moshe as he left the beach.

Suzanne suggested she and Tom go to her room and review Tom's expenses.

As Tom and Suzanne strolled to her room, she placed her arm in his. Tom looked down at her arm for a second and kept walking.

Once they arrived, Tom handed Suzanne a slip from his notebook.

"Here's my tally so far," Tom said.

Suzanne did a quick scan and placed it on the coffee table. She turned to Tom.

"It looks fine, Tommy. But I want to ask you about Moshe."

"What about Moshe?" asked Tom.

"Well, he's strange. He seems to be taking charge of this operation. What do you know about him?"

"He was recommended to me by a friend, that's all I know."

"You hired a stranger knowing nothing about his credentials? What's wrong with you. He could be in on this. I don't trust him. I think you should fire him," demanded Suzanne.

"Listen to me. Moshe was recommended by a very close friend. If Holly said he's the man I need to get this done, then that's fine with me."

"But what makes Holly an expert?"

"Look, you asked me to find Michael. And that's what I am going to do. I'm going to use everything and everyone at my disposal. If Holly says I need him, that's all I need to know. I trust Holly with my life."

"I'm sorry I brought it up. This is strange to me, not being in complete control. I'm just so worried about Michael," said Suzanne as she pulled out her hankie.

Tom put his arms around Suzanne. "It'll be fine. Don't worry, we'll find him."

She placed her head on his shoulder.

"I gotta go before I do something I'll regret," said Tom as he turned and left the room.

As Tom left the Omni, he passed a store window and noticed Scarface's reflection. A quick look around the marina and there was Tattoo but at a different location. Moshe had said, "*When you see them, that's a good thing,*" so Tom had stopped worrying. But he did quicken his pace as he returned to the *My Fortune.*

Meanwhile, back on the *My Fortune*, Moshe called the Israeli Consulate in New York. He gave his name and asked to speak to the cultural attaché.

"Moshe Kaplan, how long has it been?"

"Too long, Ira. Congratulations on your posting."

"Thank you. It's been a long time coming."

"I know, but you deserve it."

"Everyone here still talks about how you prevented that ISIS attack on New York City."

"Old news," advised Moshe. "Ira, I need your help."

"Anything. What can I do?"

"I need a clandestine operation. Can you handle it?"

"Sure, I'll do it personally. I'm getting bored here, just going to these diplomatic receptions. It's like I'm a decoration or something."

Moshe laughed. "I know exactly what you mean. This assignment is in Newport. You need to discreetly enter a house and retrieve a million dollars from the safe and send it to me in Mexico."

"OK, where in Mexico?"

"I'm staying in Puerto Aventuras, about an hour south of Cancun."

"We don't have an embassy there, but I can ship it in a US diplomatic pouch to the US consulate in Cancun. You'll have to pick it up."

"No problem."

After completing the arrangements to have the money transported, he decided to make another call to his old friend, Jonathan Long. Long was the Deputy Director for the CIA and had been a career clandestine operations specialist. During that period, Moshe had assisted him in various operations in Afghanistan, including extracting him from a life-threatening situation. He made one last local call to another friend who was in Mexico.

Tom boarded the *My Fortune,* headed straight to the bar and poured himself a Johnny Walker Black. Taking a slug, he plopped on the sofa.

"How'd your meeting go?" asked Moshe.

"Fine."

"So, what's eating at you?"

"That Suzanne is a fine looking woman. Anyone would be lucky to have her for a wife. Why would you leave someone as vivacious as that? I know I would never leave her side."

"I think you have an infatuation with her. That could lead to trouble, my friend."

"Last night, I had a dream. I was consoling the grieving widow. The bed was wet when I awoke."

"Tom, she's not what she seems."

"You're jealous of my relationship with her."

"It's just a business relationship. That's all it is, all it's ever going to be."

"Fuck you," answered Tom, storming into his bedroom.

Exactly forty-eight hours later, Tom Walker, Moshe Kaplan, and Suzanne Summerfield were seated at the table in the cabin on the *My Fortune,* staring at three suitcases containing the one million dollars. Tom began fidgeting with his string. Suzanne was busy twisting a strand of hair on the side of her head. Moshe was sitting still, quietly staring at the other two.

"What about the other two hundred fifty thousand dollars you promised?" asked Tom.

"We never had the time to get the additional money. Don't worry, Franco will take what we give him," said Moshe.

A ring tone from Suzanne's cell broke the trance. Suzanne picked up the cell phone.

"Hello."

"This is Generalissimo Franco. You have the money?"

"Yes, w…w-hat's the location?" Suzanne could barely speak.

"The GPS location is 22⁰ N 12.58" 59' by 85⁰ W 19.50" 56'."

"Sorry, I don't understand those numbers," tears began to appear in Suzanne's eyes.

"Senora, how will you get to the location?" Franco yelled out in frustration.

"Here's my captain." She started to pass the phone to Tom, but Moshe grabbed it instead.

"Who am I talking to?" questioned Moshe in a commanding voice.

"Generalissimo Alfonso Franco, leader of the Alpha 66 army of resistance."

"Who are you?" Franco demanded.

"I am Moshe Kaplan, and I will be handling the transfer from this point on."

"She was told not to tell anyone, no police. She did not do as ordered."

"I am not the police. I am Mrs. Summerfield's representative. For her safety, she will not be there at the transfer. You will have to talk to me if you want your money. We want to complete this in the best possible way with no one getting hurt."

"Fine, but I warn you, if you do not do as I say, she will not see her husband alive again."

"Of course. Understood. Now repeat the coordinates." Franco repeated the GPS coordinates.

Moshe wrote down the coordinates and handed them over to Tom. Tom shook his head up and down.

"What time are we to meet?" Moshe continued.

"Nine at night. We will not have lights but will flash a light three times every five minutes. If you see the signal, you repeat it back to me. The money must be in twenty-dollar bills."

"Impossible, we could not get past Mexican customs with that many twenties. It would take five suitcases. You will get one half in twenties and the remainder in hundreds. Unless you want to wait for us to start changing the hundreds, which could take at least a week."

"No. We take it, as you said. But if you try to cheat us, you will not see the lovely beach again."

"Understood," agreed Moshe, "we'll be waiting for your signal."

Franco disconnected. Moshe walked outside and started making calls. Moshe's call making was interrupted by a call from Miami. It was Gonzales.

"I have important information for you. You are dealing with a very deranged man. This is not the first time he has taken a hostage for ransom. He is responsible for torturing his hostages, and none has ever lived."

"Where did you get this information?" questioned Moshe.

"One of my men, Rafael Garcia, was a member of Omega 7, another Cuban resistance group working out of New Jersey. He worked with this Alfonso character. Omega 7 had used him for an operation in which they ordered him to bring the hostage to them alive. The hostage was delivered alive, but only lived for an hour after. Alfonso cut off his fingers and his balls. The man could not speak. Alfonzo cut out the man's tongue. I don't think he expects to let you or your friend leave."

"That's not good to hear."

"I will send Rafael with you. He knows Alfonso, and perhaps if this Michael is still alive, he can persuade Alfonso to release him unharmed."

"I suppose I have no choice."

"Good, then it will be so. Rafael will arrive tomorrow."

After Moshe hung up Tom asked, "Who was that? You have that look?"

"What look?"

"Like something is not going according to your plan."

"This Gonzales believes this transfer is going to go bad."

Moshe explained what Gonzales had said about past hostages when dealing with Alfonso and that he was sending one of his men to help.

"He's giving us an extra man?" questioned Tom.

"Yes, but I sense something else behind it. Let's not let our guard down when this Rafael character gets here."

"Got it," answered Tom.

"Tom, will you take me back to my hotel?" asked Suzanne.

"Of course."

At the hotel, she invited Tom up to her room for a nightcap.

RED LIPS

"Here, Tommy, sit here on the sofa," she said as she handed him a scotch neat.

She cozied up to him on the sofa.

"I'm worried. I don't like what Moshe said about this Alfonso guy. Do you think he can be trusted?"

"As Moshe said, we're not trusting anyone at this point. We'll be prepared for whatever happens," assured Tom.

"I love my husband. But I want him back in one piece. If that's not possible, don't you join him. Understand."

"I understand, but that's not going to happen. Everything will work out. Trust me."

"I am."

"Now get some rest, tomorrow will be a big day," said Tom as he left.

Back at the *My Fortune*, Tom told Moshe about the discussion with Suzanne.

"She's worried what this Alfonso guy will do to her husband," said Tom.

Moshe smiled. "Don't worry. We're in control, and I won't let anything happen to Mr. Summerfield. If he's alive at the meeting, we'll bring him back that way. What happens next is their business."

CHAPTER TWENTY

CUBA

A statuesque woman in tight jeans with a white cotton blouse draped over her bare shoulders and wearing a floppy red straw hat strolled along the dock. Her black stiletto heeled shoes getting caught between the dock planks.

"Suzanne, what are you doing here?" asked a shocked Tom.

"I've decided to join you." She turned to Moshe. "After all, I suspect I would be the first person Michael would want to see when he's released."

"Sorry, Mrs. Summerfield, but I can't let you join us. We'll call as soon as he's safe and you can meet us at the dock," ordered Moshe.

"But..."

"No. It's too dangerous. You would just put Michael and us in more danger."

"But I insist," she demanded. She stamped her foot on the dock. The heel caught between the planks and broke off.

"Not negotiable," answered Moshe, as he turned his back.

Suzanne left in a huff as she picked up the broken shoe and walked barefooted back to the hotel.

RED LIPS

Tom turned to Moshe and tried to convince him into taking Suzanne. But Moshe wouldn't budge.

General Gonzales' man, Rafael, arrived as they were preparing to depart. He was about six foot. His head was shaved high and tight, military fashion. Even in his late fifties, he was still an intimidating figure. An asset to the team, perhaps.

It was 3:30 p.m. when *My Fortune* pulled away from the dock in Puerto Aventuras. The seas were calm, but they were heading towards menacing clouds on the horizon. Tom set course at 95 degrees in an easterly direction. Sundown was at 7:30 p.m. giving them sunlight for a good portion of the trip.

"Why did you refuse to take Suzanne with us? I was surprised when she asked to join us. Perhaps she could be of some help. Michael would be pleased to see her, I'm sure," said Tom.

"Me too. But look at the way she's dressed. She's not prepared for what we are about to face. We're not going to a cotillion. There's no room for error in this situation. All she brings to the table are problems. We have enough as it stands."

Moshe looked back at Rafael, fiddling with his weapon. "And I still don't know if that's a problem or not."

"I don't know why she wanted to join us, but I know it was not in Michael's interests. Something else is going on, but I can't figure out what it is. In any case, it could turn messy, and I would rather not to have to worry about her at that moment," replied Moshe. "How are we doing on time?"

"We'll be there in plenty of time. It should take about four and a half hours, possibly five, if the wind picks up. That still gets us to the rendezvous point no later than 8:30 p.m."

"Good. I don't want Franco getting panicked and doing something stupid."

"Do you have a gun?" Moshe asked Tom.

"Yeah, I have a .357 Magnum in my stateroom, a gift from an old friend."

"What about you?"

"I'm always armed," answered Moshe as he checked out his 22 caliber Beretta.

"Kinda small," said Tom waving his Magnum.

"It's not how big your gun is but what you can do with it."

There was no need to ask Rafael, who had an AK-47 slung over his shoulder.

"Rafael, you'd better secure that piece for now. It won't be needed just yet."

"*Si,*" answered Rafael as he placed the rifle in the storage closet.

Moshe asked, "What can you tell us about this Alfonso character?"

"I was with him some years ago when he was dealing with a similar situation. Alfonso was not shy about using severe methods to achieve his goals. It will all depend on how cooperative your friend is," assured Rafael.

"Won't they search us and find our guns?" asked Tom as he checked the shells in his revolver.

"They'll know we have weapons. They'll have their own."

They continued the journey, as the sea finally swallowed the sun behind them. Darkness snuck in except for the sprinkle of stars visible past the clouds back towards Cancun.

"I'll have to turn off our running lights as we get close to our destination. There'll be patrol boats searching the area. It's dark tonight, going to be hard to see."

"I know. That's in our favor," replied Moshe.

Moshe was dressed all in black. Black sneakers, black jeans, and a black t-shirt. He turned to Tom, who was dressed in light tan shorts and a white shirt, "Don't you have something darker in your wardrobe?"

"Of course, do I need it?"

"Only if you don't want to be a target. This could go bad, and I wouldn't want to drive this thing back myself."

"Oh! You made a funny. Take the helm, Moshe, while I change."

Tom returned in a black Metallica sweatshirt, tuxedo pants and shoes, and a yarmulke (skullcap).

Moshe took one look and started laughing. "OK! I give up. Where did you get that outfit?"

"The sweatshirt at a yard sale, pants, and shoes from my last wedding in 1985 and the skullcap from a Bat Mitzvah I attended a few years back. Why? Don't you like it?"

"It's you," was all Moshe could say.

A strong wind picked up from the north, the sky darkened, and heavy seas caused the *My Fortune* to roll. The sudden gale had caught them by surprise.

Tom was fighting the wheel but unable to keep on course. The storm forced him to steer into the wind to keep the *My Fortune* from floundering.

The boat rose up the face of the wave and broke through the crest, then down the backside. Everyone was holding on. Rafael attempted to make it to the head but heaved his dinner over the floor anyway. Moshe felt sorry for him, but Tom started laughing. He had been in this type of weather many times and enjoyed the challenge.

Rafael went out to the deck, thinking he would feel better. Rain caused the floor to become slippery, and Rafael was having a difficult time keeping his balance. His hands turned white, clasping the railing. But there was never any doubt Tom would get them to their destination. After all, he was an expert seaman, at home on the seas.

"Where's the life jackets?" yelled the now pale Rafael.

"In the cabin under the bench," Tom shouted. "Why don't you lay down. We'll call you when it's time."

Rafael stumbled down into the cabin.

The gale had subsided a bit, and Tom attempted to get back on course. Heavy rain continued, and swells kept the boat rocking, but the danger had passed for the moment.

"Moshe, we got company," said Tom, looking up from the radar screen.

"Where?" asked Moshe.

"Coming off our stern."

Moshe asked for the binoculars. Tom grabbed a set that hung by the wheel and handed them to Moshe.

"Tom, how's it moving?" asked Moshe.

"Fast and straight for us. I saw it a while ago, but then it disappeared."

Moshe walked out to the back deck and looked through the binoculars.

Moshe thought he saw something but wasn't sure. He kept looking.

He cleaned off the binoculars and took another look. "I thought I saw something on the horizon for a second."

"It's still following," said Tom. "it comes and goes off the radar. But it looks close."

A few minutes later, he was sure.

"Yes. It's a boat following us."

"What kind?" asked Tom.

"Well, can't tell yet, but it seems like a rum-runner or cigarette boat. Running low in the water. I'll keep an eye on it."

"You could be right. In these seas, it would be on and off my radar screen," confirmed Tom.

And Moshe watched for thirty minutes. Sure enough, it kept following.

"I don't like it. Do you think it's Franco?" asked Tom.

"No, Tom. It's too far out for him. Besides, she's coming from the wrong direction."

Just then, Rafael appeared from the cabin with his life jacket, a flare gun, and his AK-47.

"Please stop the boat, Captain," ordered Rafael as he fired the flare into the night sky.

A cigarette boat almost the same size as the *My Fortune* appeared with Gonzales and four of his men. They pulled up to the port side.

"What's going on, Rafael?" asked Moshe.

"Nothing for you to worry about as long as you give us the money you are carrying."

The boat pulled along the port side. In the rough waters, Gonzales found it a challenge to board *My Fortune*. But he was able to grab hold of the rail and lift himself aboard.

"Gentlemen, so glad to see you. I hope you have the money. I will make this as painless as possible."

"Why?" Tom asked.

"This money will help us restart the revolution in Cuba. You will be heroes. We will build a monument for you in Havana," answered Gonzales. He broke out in laughter. "Of course, if you don't comply with my… shall we say request, you will not be around to see it."

Gonzales yelled out for his man, "Alexandro bring the boat alongside." But the rough seas and heavy rain would not oblige.

"Alexandro come here. Stop fucking around," screamed an agitated Gonzales.

Moshe stood on the starboard side with the AK-47 pointed directly at him, no more than a yard away. Tom was on the port side next to Gonzales, holding on to the railing.

"Toss me the line, and I'll pull you in," yelled out Gonzales.

As Alexandro attempted to throw the rope, Gonzales leaned over the rail. The raindrops pelted his eyes. He wiped his face and missed the line. Moshe was tense watching the scene as Rafael kept aim at him with the AK-47. A second try was successful, but as Gonzales leaned over and grabbed the line, a wave crashed over the starboard side, raising the port side into the air.

Rafael was unprepared, and as he attempted to grab the railing, Moshe caught him by the crotch and heaved him overboard with one hand. The AK-47 was of no help.

RED LIPS

Tom took his cue, and with only a nudge, Gonzales joined Rafael. Without a life vest, Gonzales found it challenging to stay afloat. Alexandro, on the floundering cigarette boat, attempted to pluck Gonzales out of the horrific seas. Rafael was on his own.

"Tom! Start the engine, and let's get the hell out of here," yelled Moshe.

"What about them?" said Tom pointing to the floundering cigarette boat. "What if they follow us?"

"They'll have trouble navigating these waves with that boat. I don't think she'll catch up to us."

"But she's sinking?"

"Not our problem," answered Moshe.

As they pulled away, the cigarette boat and Gonzales disappeared, but Tom still saw the bright orange speck bobbing on the ocean.

CHAPTER TWENTY-ONE

MICHAEL'S RESCUE

The rain subsided as the storm passed. The *My Fortune* was on plane as it sped through the waves. Tom's twenty-odd years as a charter captain paid off. He focused on making up the lost minutes.

They arrived at their destination fifteen minutes late. Tom felt the twitching in his stomach. He didn't know whether he would have diarrhea or heave up his lunch. Thankfully, he'd skipped dinner.

Tom retrieved his flashlight from the cabin and flashed it three times as agreed. There was no response. Five minutes later, he tried again. Same results. It was not looking good, but they tried flashing one more time. They looked for a signal, but there was none. As a last recourse, Tom hit the boat's running lights twice. A few moments later, blinking lights flashed in the distance. They waited silently, looking. Five minutes later, there were three more light flashes. Moshe took the flashlight and turned it on and off three times. Five minutes later, he repeated the signal and waited.

Slowly, out of the darkness, appeared a small fishing boat. The boat moved closer and revealed its crew of three men in fatigues and a fourth in civilian clothes. Two of the men had automatic rifles pointed at Tom and Moshe. The boat pulled alongside.

"*Generalissimo, vengan a bordo, por favor,*" shouted Moshe as he opened the rear gate to the deck of the *My Fortune.*

A scowling Franco stepped on to the boat.

"You are late. What took you so long? Where's the money?" Franco demanded.

"Where's Michael?" responded an unintimidated Moshe.

"Oh, yes. Bring Mr. Summerfield," he commanded in Spanish to one of the men still on the fishing boat.

Michael stepped on board without any assistance. His clothes were wrinkled but clean. Not what Moshe had expected from someone who was a hostage.

"How are you, Michael?" questioned Moshe.

"I'm well. I was well taken care of by my saviors."

"What do you mean saviors?" a startled look appeared on Tom's face.

"My boat blew up, and these kind fishermen plucked me out of the ocean. Thought I would die. I'd been drifting on a small dinghy for three days with no water or food when they found me. They were kind enough to hide me from the government troops and call Suzanne."

"We are wasting time, where is my money?" Franco repeated.

Moshe marched into the cabin, followed by the second fisherman with the rifle, and retrieved a suitcase. He placed it in front of Franco. Franco looked at it and ordered Michael to open it. Michael complied. The bag opened with no incident. Nothing exploded red dye over everything. Franco examined the money. There were US twenty-dollar bills but no 100's.

"This is not what we discussed," an angry Franco yelled out.

"What did you expect to do with all that money in Cuba? You're a hunted man," continued Moshe in a calming voice.

"We will use that money to bribe officials. That will allow us to escape to Mexico and, hopefully, to America."

Just then, a shell exploded alongside the boats. Franco and his men ran back to the fishing boat with the money, believing a Cuban gunboat had spotted them. Moshe threw Tom and Michael to the ground. Bullets flew over them as the bandits escaped.

Suddenly, a large grey hulled military vessel approached from out of the black. It displayed no nation's flag. A loud bullhorn screamed, "Are you OK?"

Moshe shouted back, "Yes, A-OK."

The US destroyer lowered a red rigid-hulled inflatable motorboat, with three men aboard. It pulled alongside the *My Fortune*. Moshe smiled as Jonathan Long boarded.

"Anyone hurt?" Jonathan questioned.

"No, Jon. We're all fine."

"Stop! No names, Moshe, I'm not here."

"Sorry. You were a little late. Where were you?"

"We had to evade a Cuban patrol boat. What happened here?" asked Jon.

"Franco took the money and ran as soon as they heard the shell. I think they thought you were the Cuban patrol boat."

"And no one was hurt, Moshe?"

"They fired some rounds, but they looked like they were trying to scare us. All the rounds were fired over our heads."

"Lucky for you."

"I don't think they had any intention of doing any of us any harm. From what I heard from Michael Summerfield, the hostage, they saved his life and treated him very well."

"You gave them the money?" asked Jonathan as his jaw almost hit the ground in disbelief.

"No, not all, just 250 thousand." Moshe motioned Jon into the cabin. "The rest is still here," continued Moshe as he pointed to the additional suitcases.

"I guess they deserve something for saving an American."

Moshe laughed, "Cheap at that."

"We'll follow you out of Cuban waters until you're safe."

"No, I don't think it will be necessary, but I appreciate the offer, and thanks again."

"We're even," replied a smiling Jonathan.

"No, I owe you." Moshe waved goodbye as the destroyer pulled away.

On the way back to Mexican waters, they huddled in the wheelhouse. Michael explained how the fisherman had picked him up. "He asked me what I was doing out here alone. But I couldn't understand him at the time. I asked if he spoke English, and he responded, 'No.'

"The man spoke no English for the rest of the trip. I was so weak he needed to assist me in getting into his boat. Next, he gave me a small sip of water and a piece of his sandwich. He pulled up a sail, and we sailed back to his village. It took half a day. Back at the village, we met with a man who spoke English, Alfonso Franco. I told my story of how my boat had blown up, and I was adrift for three days. I wanted to thank the man for saving me and would reward him well. They sheltered me in a small hut for the night."

"By the way, is there anything to drink on board?" asked Michael. "Except rum, that's all I had for the last month."

"Sure," answered Tom. I have scotch, gin, vodka, cognac, wine, beer."

"Beer would be great."

Tom handed him a beer from the fridge.

Michael took a swig and continued, "The next morning, I woke refreshed. Overnight I realized Suzanne's business sense would never allow me to give this man the one million dollars I thought he deserved. There was probably a problem with the Cuban officials bringing in that much foreign currency anyway. You know, confiscate most of it in taxes, etc. I devised a plan. That was when I had Alfonso make the call. I'm sorry it caused so much trouble for you. I thought it would be a simple transfer."

"I understand," said Tom.

"They just wanted to get out of Cuba," added Michael.

"I may be able to help with that," offered Moshe.

A flash of light over the horizon, followed by the sound of a cannon's roar and a splash of water spilling over the bow, canceled the celebration.

"Tom," yelled Moshe, "get us out of here."

RED LIPS

Tom rammed the throttle forward and put the *My Fortune* on plane immediately. A zigzag course followed, trying to evade the shelling as another landed near the stern.

"Who's shooting at us?" asked Michael.

"It must be the Cuban gunboat my friend mentioned. I should have taken him up on that offer to escort us."

"Too late, shut off the lights," shouted Tom.

But the shells kept coming, and they could now see the silhouette of the approaching patrol boat, not boat... boats.

"Shit! There are two of them," barked Tom.

"How far are we from getting out of Cuban waters?" Moshe asked.

"We're out, but they're not stopping."

Two more shells hit on either side of the boat, causing the rear deck to flood.

"Moshe! Get the life jackets from under the sofa."

They all put on their life jackets in preparation for abandoning the boat.

Just then, another flash from a different direction appeared, but no shell hit near them. Then another and another. Still no splash.

Then they heard the noise. That familiar loud horn. The welcomed grey unflagged destroyer.

Jonathan's voice came over the radio. "You guys, alright?"

"Yes, thanks to you. I thought you weren't going to escort us?" said Tom.

"We weren't, but we saw the flash and figured you might be in trouble."

"I think I'll take you up on your offer to escort us this time."

"You got it."

On the way back, they stayed huddled in the wheelhouse.

"Captain Walker, I think it's time for something stronger than beer," announced Michael.

"I have an unopened bottle of Johnny Walker Blue."

"That'll work."

"Moshe, can you take the wheel?"

Tom poured two glasses of the Blue and one Stoli for Moshe.

"How did Suzanne look?" asked Michael.

"She's fine. Worried about you," Tom lied.

"Our marriage has been on rocky ground the last year or so. There have been money issues since I left the plant. There were some secrets that I couldn't confide to Suzanne. But, after what has transpired and her taking the initiative to find and hire you two, I think that we'll be fine. Thank you both."

"You're welcome," answered Tom.

"Captain are you an honest man?" inquired Michael.

"I believe I am. At least I try to be."

"Do you believe in karma?"

"Yes, definitely."

"Me too," Michael responded.

"Why all the questions."

"I believe faith put us together, and good karma saved us for a purpose."

"What purpose is that?" asked Tom.

"Not now. That's for another time and place," answered Michael.

CHAPTER TWENTY-TWO

MICHAEL'S HOMECOMING

Michael's calls to Suzanne were a fool's errand. As they approached Puerto Aventuras, Michael tried calling Suzanne several times, but it kept going to voicemail. He left messages advising their estimated time of arrival of approximately two in the morning.

Suzanne was nowhere in sight when they pulled into the dock. They tied up the boat, and Michael rushed off, anxious to see if Suzanne was waiting. That was when the fireworks started — two shots flashed in the night, followed by a third. Then silence.

Moshe pulled Michael back onto the boat. But not before Michael took one in the shoulder. Tom searched for his Magnum and took cover on the deck. Tattoo appeared out of the darkness. Moshe stopped Tom from shooting him just in time.

"It's OK, Tom. He's one of us," yelled out Moshe, before he checked Michael's wound. "You'll be fine. Just grazed you."

"I have injured man here, need help comrade," yelled Tattoo in his heavy Ukrainian accent.

Moshe ran out and assisted his friend. They dragged Scarface back to the boat, blood dripping from his leg.

Michael ran out of the cabin. "What's going on?"

"This man's been following Tom since he began looking for you. I believe he's a hitman contracted by someone who wants you dead. Who do you think that could be?" asked Moshe.

"Could be the oil companies," offered Michael.

"I don't think so. They have sophisticated ways of eliminating people, such as poisons, etc. Besides, he took a shot at me awhile back."

"How do you know?" asked Tom.

"Illya saw him get the two shots off and run." Moshe turned his attention to Scarface, "Who hired you?"

Scarface was silent. Moshe grabbed his injured leg and put his finger in the wound. He moved his finger around the hole. They heard him shriek, breaking the quiet night.

"I want a lawyer," demanded Scarface.

Moshe was hysterical, laughing.

"You think we are the police? Oh no, I am your worst nightmare. I am an unknown spirit. A spook, as they say in your country. I will disappear, and no one will know. But first, I will torture and kill you. Understand?"

A shaken Scarface realized he was in deep trouble. "What happens if I tell?"

"We leave you at the hospital. I will follow-up with the person or persons who hired you, and I promise they will not come after you after I finish with them. Now, do we continue, or are you ready to talk?" demanded Moshe.

"I'll talk. But, look, it was just a job. She offered a great deal of money. You understand?"

"Yes, but who hired you?"

"Suzanne Summerfield hired me to follow the Captain. She never expected him to find her husband, just needed someone to testify he was dead."

"Why did you shoot at me?" asked Moshe.

"She felt you were too good and thought I could scare you off the assignment."

Illya's brow came together, his lips became taut as he looked over at Moshe. Moshe looked back and nodded up and down.

"And what about Michael?" continued Moshe

"If the Captain found him, I was to eliminate the problem. She needed him out of the way to sell some patents. Look, man, it was just a job. I have a wife and children."

"Yeah, I bet," Moshe pulled out his Beretta and fired one round into Scarface's head.

Illya picked up Scarface by the seat of his pants and dragged him to the car and left.

Tom started running around the deck, flaring his hands over his head. "You promised you would take him to the hospital," screamed Tom.

"Yes, and Illya will drop him in front of the hospital as promised. Never give someone a second chance to kill you. Not in my business. He was no amateur. He was a professional assassin. His reputation was tarnished. He wouldn't stop until he'd finished the job. And that includes the people I care about most. Do you understand? This is my world."

A calmer Tom Walker answered, "You're right. Your world is one I'm not familiar with."

"But what about Suzanne?" Tom continued.

Moshe looked over at a pale Michael. "Let me dress that wound for you."

Tom brought out the first aid kit.

Moshe cleaned and dressed the wound.

"There that looks better. How's it feel?"

"Fine. I need a drink." Michael proceeded into the galley and poured himself a water glass full of scotch. After a few gulps, he sat, took a deep breath, and stated. "I'll handle this myself. I thought this might happen. I know what to do. This problem will not change my plan. Can I sleep here tonight?"

"Of course," replied Tom.

"You can have my suite, I'm finished here, and I have an important date in Newport," offered Moshe as he picked up his duffle bag and heaved it on the dock. "Illya will be back and pick me up. Meanwhile, I think I'll join Michael. Do you have any more Stoli?"

"Of course," said Tom as he opened the refrigerator and handed the bottle to Moshe.

Not to be outdone, Tom poured himself a Johnny Walker Blue and, putting it up to his lips, yelled, "Cheers."

"*Nostrovia,*" said Moshe. "Tom, I must admit this was an interesting week. But it's time for me to leave."

"Before you leave, I need to know who you are? You owe me that," asked Tom.

"My name doesn't matter. All you need to know is I'm a retired assassin for the Mossad."

"Why did you retire?"

"I resented being an assassin."

"But you just killed a man."

"Yes. But that was personal."

"And who's that big guy with all the tattoos? I thought he was one of them."

"Illya is a retired agent for Interpol. I was introduced to him while working on a case in New York. He worked undercover on the same case in Kyiv. We stopped a terrorist attempt. ISIS was planning an attack on New York City. Since then, he works for me from time to time."

"Will I see you again," asked Captain Tom.

"Probably not. But one never knows, does one? If you need me, call Holly. You have her number."

Moments later, Moshe was walking to Illya's waiting car.

Tom yelled, "Give my love to Holly."

Moshe did not turn back to Tom but raised his right hand and gave it a thumbs-up as he walked away into the night.

The next morning, Michael was preparing to leave.

"What was your arrangement with Suzanne?" Michael asked

"Don't worry about it. I just enjoyed the adventure. But I'm afraid there is Moshe's fee."

"Nonsense," Michael opened the suitcase and took out two thousand dollars, "Spending money, the rest is yours and Moshe's."

They shook hands.

"You'll be hearing from me in a year or two. Be prepared for a short trip," said Michael.

Tom wished him well and did not expect to see Suzanne again.

With everyone gone and nothing left for Tom, he decided to go to Manny's. *Perhaps Beverly Mount will be there.*

CHAPTER TWENTY-THREE

BELIZE

The call came eighteen months later. Tom was on the phone with Sally. She called him at least once a week since he reconciled with his children and four new grandchildren, two girls and two boys, last year.

"Sorry, I have another call. Call me next week. Love you."

Sally responded, "Love you too, Dad, next week then."

Tom took Michael's call. Michael was now living in Belize on Ambergris Caye.

"Hello."

"Hi Tom, It's Michael Summerfield."

"Michael. Where have you been hiding? How are you?"

"I'm living in Belize. Doing great. How about getting off your ass and taking a trip down here?"

Tom's curiosity piqued.

"You know that is not a bad idea. I am trying to get out more. When?"

"How 'bout tomorrow?" answered Michael.

"Let's make it next week. I'll take the *My Fortune* for a spin. Time to get it moving anyway. Hey, mind if I bring Mr. Tibbs?"

"Who's that?"

"My dog."

"You have a dog? What kind?"

"Chocolate Lab," answered Tom.

"Sure. No problem. Bring him."

Arrangements were made. One week later, the *My Fortune* pulled into the Belize Yacht Club Marina in San Pedro.

Mr. Tibbs and Tom were met by Michael, who whisked them off to his oceanfront villa. During the ride, Mr. Tibbs kept his head out the window, enjoying the breeze.

"When did you acquire your friend?"

"About a year ago. He was wandering around, lost. I couldn't locate the owner, so I took him in. The vet says he is part lab about six years old. Loves the beach and the water."

They drove into the long driveway of a large villa. No, not a villa, a mansion.

At three stories with an orange Spanish-tiled roof and stucco walls, it was possibly the tallest building on the Caye, it could have been the Governor's Mansion.

They entered through the double teak front doors. Michael directed Tom to one of the upstairs bedrooms. After dropping his luggage off in one of the second-floor suites, he met with Michael in the downstairs library. The walls were filled with books, more than both Tom and Michael could read in five years.

Michael poured two tumblers of Johnny Walker and Sons Odyssey Blended Malt scotch. Not the most expensive scotch in the world, but at $1000 a bottle, close enough. They cheered to their good fortune.

"So, Michael, why'd you ask me to come? I know it wasn't to share a drink of scotch."

Michael walked up to three suitcases sitting on top of a table.

"I have some unfinished business which I feel needs to be addressed face to face," answered Michael as he opened one of the suitcases revealing $1,000,000 in cash. "There's another million in each of the others."

"Holy shit, what's that for?"

"I have a proposition for you."

"What's that?" Tom was getting the feeling he was being hooked again.

"I want you to take this money and personally give it to my daughter Marie."

"Why not do it yourself or send her a check?"

"Because, if I leave Belize, the US authorities will arrest me."

"What for?"

"Fraud."

"I don't understand."

Michael took another sip of his drink and explained that after the Cuban incident, he divorced Suzanne. She had accepted a simple one million dollar settlement rather than be charged with attempted murder. He then sold his patent for his engine to an oil lobbyist representing the major oil companies for twenty million dollars. Five of which Michael gave his ex-wife, who had sabotaged his boat. The argument they had on the yacht was because she kept pushing Michael to sell his patent and he refused. She figured with him dead, she could sell the patent on her own.

"But you were divorced?"

"True, but Marie gets fifty percent of my estate, and Dorothy has control of Marie."

"I see. So, you end up with fifteen million give or take with the house and everything, being that Suzanne didn't get it."

"Not Exactly. Suzanne kept the house. It was her's before we married. But I'm not greedy, besides there is still plenty for me."

"That still does not explain why I need to give Marie the money in cash, personally."

"Because if the government finds out the money is from me, they will confiscate it."

"I'm bewildered."

"I stole the money from the oil companies, and they want it back," Michael laughed as he tried to continue. "They have already confiscated the five million from Dorothy."

With tears of laughter in his eyes, he stated, "Isn't that great restitution?"

"I think you're crazy," Tom confessed.

"No. Shrewd. The oil companies tried to stop me, but I got the last laugh."

"How?"

"The patent's no good. The engine doesn't work, never did."

"But you sailed to Key West on only two gallons of gas."

"I had twin bladders with 100 gallons of fuel in each hidden in the bilge of the boat."

"So, this was your plan all along?"

"Yes, and there's an extra million for you if you accept this challenge."

"Why you old coot. It'll be a pleasure to do this for you. But I'll do it for no charge. You overpaid me the last time"

RED LIPS

They finished the bottle of scotch.

EPILOGUE

After much pleading, Marie agreed to meet Tom. She was living in a small condo in Newport.

"Marie, I am a friend of your father."

"I told you I do not want anything to do with my father," said Marie throwing out her hands.

"I know but hear me out. This is important. Your father loves you. He always has. I'm here to turn over a large sum of money to you."

"I understand. But I don't want my father's money. He hurt my mother, and I'll never forgive him for that," Marie replied. She folded her hands across her chest.

Tom realized this would be harder than he thought. He hadn't expected her to refuse the money.

"Marie, your father made some serious mistakes, as we all do. But he is trying to make amends. Remember, your mother tried to kill him, and if not for the fisherman who plucked him out of the ocean, we would not even be having this conversation."

Tom thought, *Was I being too direct, too cold? I have a way of losing empathy for others when conducting business.*

"I strongly suggest you reconsider. You can always share your fortune with your mother if you wish."

Marie was silent. She pulled on her earlobe with her right hand.

Tom sat and stared, not knowing what else to say.

RED LIPS

" OK. I'm listening. Go on." Marie broke the stalemate.

"He asked me to arrange the transfer of three million dollars to you. But I'm afraid there will be consequences if I hand it over."

"I understand. So how can you do that without bringing it to the attention of the government?"

"I have a great deal of money of my own, and what I plan to do is set up a trust fund for you with my funds."

"But how will you get it back?"

"Easy, I will systematically make deposits to myself gradually. I am constantly transferring funds from one account to another. Residing in Mexico, the government would not even notice one or two extras."

"And I can share it with my mother?"

"If you wish. The money is yours."

She was quiet for some time. Finally, she turned to Tom.

"Then, let's do it."

Three months later, Marie had a three-million-dollar trust fund. She began receiving payments soon after and did share her fortune with her mother. She never told her mother where the money came from and sent just enough to help support her. Dorothy Summerfield died a few months later of cirrhosis of the liver.

Neither Captain Tom Walker nor Michael Summerfield ever heard again from Marie.

CAST OF CHARACTERS

Order of Appearance

Manuel (Manny) Sanchez, owner of Papacito's Cocina Mexicanos and Tom Walker's best friend

Beverly Mount widowed cougar on the prowl for Tom

Holly Flynn

Moshe Kaplan

Generalissimo Alfonso Franco Cuban Alpha 66

General Gonzales, Miami Alpha 66

Johnathan Long, CIA

CREDITS

Poem: Red Lipstick by Gabriella permission applied for.

Tom Ogle   El Paso Times, by John Doussard

Paul Pantone – Stanley Allen Meyer at

References

Paul Pantone, Tom Ogle, and Stanley Allen Meyer and various sources.

Note: any conspiracy theories are strictly speculation and cannot be proven. But it makes for a good story of fiction.